*A Candlelight
Ecstasy Romance®*

"LET'S HAVE DINNER AGAIN TOMORROW EVENING," JON SAID.

Michelle shook her head. "I don't think so, Jon. We should keep our relationship professional."

"Why?"

"I just don't think it would be good for us to get involved in a personal relationship."

"I think it could be very good for both of us," he murmured, his eyes holding hers. "When we met for the first time yesterday, I felt a chemistry between us. You felt it, too. Admit it."

"Well, maybe I did feel something, but . . ."

"Then how about dinner?"

She wavered a second, then regained control of herself. "No, Jon."

"Okay, so you're stubborn. But I'm telling you now, I can be stubborn, too. When I want something, I can usually find a way to get it. Right now, I want us to get to know each other better. And I'm going to succeed."

CANDLELIGHT ECSTASY CLASSIC ROMANCES

CANDLELIGHT ECSTASY ROMANCES®

QUANTITY SALES

Most Dell Books are available at special quantity discounts when purchased in bulk by corporations, organizations, and special-interest groups. Custom imprinting or excerpting can also be done to fit special needs. For details write: Dell Publishing Co., Inc., 1 Dag Hammarskjold Plaza, New York, NY 10017, Attn.: Special Sales Dept., or phone: (212) 605-3319.

INDIVIDUAL SALES

Are there any Dell Books you want but cannot find in your local stores? If so, you can order them directly from us. You can get any Dell book in print. Simply include the book's title, author, and ISBN number, if you have it, along with a check or money order (no cash can be accepted) for the full retail price plus 75¢ per copy to cover shipping and handling. Mail to: Dell Readers Service, Dept. FM, 6 Regent Street, Livingston, N.J. 07039.

FIRST-CLASS MALE

Donna Kimel Vitek

A CANDLELIGHT ECSTASY ROMANCE®

Published by
Dell Publishing Co., Inc.
1 Dag Hammarskjold Plaza
New York, New York 10017

ISBN: 0-440-12554-5

Printed in the United States of America

May 1987

10 9 8 7 6 5 4 3 2 1

WFH

To Our Readers:

We have been delighted with your enthusiastic response to Candlelight Ecstasy Romances®, and we thank you for the interest you have shown in this exciting series.

In the upcoming months we will continue to present the distinctive sensuous love stories you have come to expect only from Ecstasy. We look forward to bringing you many more books from your favorite authors and also the very finest work from new authors of contemporary romantic fiction.

As always, we are striving to present the unique, absorbing love stories that you enjoy most—books that are more than ordinary romance. Your suggestions and comments are always welcome. Please write to us at the address below.

Sincerely,

The Editors
Candlelight Romances
1 Dag Hammarskjold Plaza
New York, New York 10017

FIRST-CLASS MALE

CHAPTER ONE

Debbie Miller came into the office and closed the door behind her.

From her desk Michelle Vance looked up at the receptionist. "What is it, Deb?"

Debbie gestured toward the door. "That attorney who made an appointment to see you is outside. He's early. Should I have him wait?"

Putting down the file she had been reading, Michelle glanced at her wristwatch, then shook her head. "Oh, he's only five minutes early. I can see him now. Please send him in."

"Gladly. Now I get to talk to him again." Debbie grinned and waggled her eyebrows up and down. "He's a real hunk, isn't he?"

Michelle chuckled. "Deb, you think most men are hunks."

"But this one really is."

"I wouldn't know. Never met Mr. Wyatt. I've seen his picture in the newspapers a couple of times. He seems to be reasonably attractive."

"Reasonably attractive! Oh, he's more than that. Wait until you see him."

"I would like to do that. Now," Michelle said wryly. "Have him come in, and you and I will rate him on a level of one to ten after I've had my meeting with him."

Stifling a giggle, the receptionist opened the door and went out.

A moment later, as Michelle was tidying the papers on her desk, Jonathan Wyatt entered the office. Standing, Michelle extended her hand. He took it; his grip was firm. "It's nice to meet you," she said, indicating a chair at the left side of the desk. "Please have a seat." As he did, she returned to her own swivel chair. "Now, what can I do to help you, Mr. Wyatt?"

"Call me Jon, please. I'm a very informal person," he said with a friendly smile as his green eyes took in her nicely shaped slender figure, wavy auburn hair, and lovely blue eyes. Then his smile deepened. "You're not at all what I expected."

Michelle met his amused gaze. "Oh? And what did you expect?"

He relaxed back in the chair. "When Arnold Evans told me you were an expert on battered women, I immediately got a mental picture of a woman in her fifties with gray hair. A middle-aged matron. You're not even a young matron, I assume. No wedding ring on your finger."

Smiling, Michelle smoothed the skirt of her navy blue suit with her ringless left hand. "I'm older than I look. And as a matter of fact, you aren't as old as I thought you were, either. I've seen your picture in the newspaper, and the camera made you look a bit more mature."

"Exactly what my mother said. She wasn't happy about it. Said my looking older made her feel older. I'm thirty-three. How old are you?"

Michelle had to laugh. "I'd heard you're good at cross-examining people, but I'm not on the witness stand. And don't you know it's not polite to ask a lady her age?"

"Even one as young as you?" he retorted, grinning.

She grinned back. "As I said, I'm older than I look; let's just leave it at that." She turned the conversation back to business. "Now, if you'll tell me what I can do for you . . ."

Jon Wyatt leaned forward in his chair. "Could we have this discussion over lunch? After our meeting I have to get right back to my office in Raleigh, and if I don't eat now, I won't have a chance. Would you mind?"

Consulting her watch once more, Michelle saw that it was eleven thirty-five. "I wouldn't mind at all. I'm getting a little hungry myself. There's a very good Italian restaurant right down the street. Do you like Italian food?"

"Love it," he said, rising to his feet.

After taking her navy clutch purse from a desk drawer, Michelle preceded Jon out of the office and asked him to wait a moment in the reception area while she went across the room. Debbie was standing at a small table pouring a cup of coffee.

"Mr. Wyatt and I are going out to lunch, Deb," said Michelle, tucking her purse under her left arm. "But I'll be back long before my one o'clock appointment."

"Oh, lunch," Deb whispered, rolling her eyes suggestively. "Sounds cozy."

"Don't be silly. It's strictly business."

"You're crazy" was Deb's teasing retort. "Take another look at the man, Michelle. About six one, sandy blond hair, fabulous green eyes, and he seems so nice. Men like that don't come around often, as we well know in this business. You'd better try to get something going with him. And he has a great build. Looks strong but not muscle-bound. He's a successful lawyer, too. He could take care of you in style, if you'd just—"

"Will you stop this nonsense?" Michelle interrupted quietly, chasing back a smile at Deb's relentless romanticism. "Just hold down the fort while I'm gone."

As Michelle started to turn away, Debbie grabbed her by the arm, her expression sobering. "I'm not joking. Mr. Wyatt is nice, and you could use a man in your life. You're working too much."

"My work is important."

"Yes, but—"

"Enough, Deb," Michelle stated firmly, setting her small jaw. "Mr. Wyatt is standing over there waiting for me, and I'm not going to stay here whispering with you. We must look like a couple of silly schoolgirls." Mildly irritated, she walked away.

"What was that powwow all about?" Jon asked as he opened the door of the small counseling center for Michelle. "Something wrong?"

"Nothing major. Deb and her boyfriend had a little tiff, and she picked now to talk to me about it," Michelle lied, turning right as they stepped outside. "The restaurant's only a few doors down this way."

Golden rays of mid-October sun washed over the university town of Chapel Hill, North Carolina. They shone on leaves that were turning orange and red and yellow, making them shimmer. On the nearly two-hundred-year-old campus, worn brick walkways meandered through lush, cropped grass that was peppered with ancient trees. Their spreading boughs provided welcome shade in summer. In winter, holly trees provided greenery.

As Michelle and Jon walked along Franklin Street across from the campus's original quadrangle of post-Revolutionary buildings, she glanced at it frequently. It was a place she loved. If they could talk, the weathered pink bricks of the old walls could tell so many stories—so many young minds had sought knowledge here.

Jon noticed her preoccupation and smiled down at her as they walked on. "The quad does have that effect on one, doesn't it? There's something special about it, if you were ever a student here. And you obviously were."

"Junior and senior years. How about you?"

"Freshman through law school."

"They must have given you a great legal education. At the relatively young age of thirty-three, you've made a reputation for yourself in Raleigh. The newspapers say you're the brightest up-and-coming attorney in town."

"Well, I am good."

"Not to mention modest," she said, smiling cheekily at him as he opened the door of the restaurant. They went in.

"I've heard you're good, too," he said after the hostess had seated them at a small candlelit table in the corner. "Best battered women expert in Orange County."

"That's me. Unfortunately, I'm the only battered women counselor in the county. I could use some help. But I doubt I'll get it anytime soon, the way the federal government's cut back on funds for social programs. It seems like missles and more missles are more—"

She didn't finish her sentence because a waiter stepped up to the table. He introduced himself as Carl and poured them glasses of ice water from a pitcher. Then he left them to peruse the menu. Michelle recommended the veal parmigiana; they both ordered it when the waiter returned several minutes later.

They took sips of water while waiting for their iced tea to be served. Putting down his glass, Jon placed his tanned hands upon the tabletop. "Here's the story. I have a client I want you to evaluate."

Michelle nodded. "A battered woman?"

"Wife. Doris Keaton is her name. She's been charged with attempted murder. She shot her husband two weeks ago."

Sighing, Michelle shook her head. "Damn, another one pushed too far. I imagine he was threatening her when she shot him."

"So she says."

Michelle frowned. "Don't you believe her?"

"That doesn't really matter. She's entitled to defense even if she's guilty."

"So that means you don't believe her?"

14

"Yes, I do, as a matter of fact. Of course, she could be lying to me. Her husband swears she is. The way he tells it, she was waiting for him when he got home and shot him. He says she was seeing another man but wouldn't get a divorce because she'd have to give up being rich. The husband's a very popular fiction author. Used to be a professor here at the university. He claims she intended to kill him to inherit his money but that he managed to run away when the first shot wasn't fatal. She claims he was coming after her with a baseball bat and she shot him in self-defense.

Michelle smiled at the waiter when he brought the iced tea. She took a sip before asking about Doris Keaton. "Tell me how she impresses you."

"Afraid of everything. Acts as if she would jump at her own shadow."

"Typical. Sounds like you might have a good case. But I'll have to talk to her several times before I can make a final judgment and swear in court that she appears to be a battered woman. Had she ever told anyone she was being beaten by her husband?"

Jon shook his head. "Said she was too ashamed to admit it."

Michelle winced. "That's typical, too, but it's too bad she didn't confide in someone. Would've made her story much more convincing."

"I know, but she didn't even tell her sister what was happening, what had been happening all the twenty-one years of her marriage. From what I hear, the husband, Vincent Keaton, is slick. A fiction writer could concoct a convincing story that a jury might just believe."

"Well, I'll try to help you make Doris's side of it very convincing, too, if I can help you at all. I'll have to see her first. I'm free between two and three tomorrow afternoon. Think she could come in to see me then?"

Rubbing his jaw, Jon shook his head. "That's a problem. You're going to have to go to her, if possible. Doris Keaton's in a very bad emotional state right now. After she shot her husband, she fell apart completely. After her sister and brother-in-law got her out of jail, they had to call Dr. Evans, a psychiatrist, to treat her for extreme withdrawal. He'll be testifying on her behalf also, but he's not an expert on battered women. He told me she's better now than she was right after the shooting, but she's still terrified of leaving her sister's house. The only time she's been out was to go to her arraignment in court."

"She's afraid her husband might attack her again?"

"Yes, although he's still in the hospital recuperating from a fairly severe shoulder wound. She's still too traumatized to be completely rational yet."

"That's understandable," murmured Michelle, her expression sympathetic. "Of course I can go see her. Will you tell her I'll be there at two o'clock tomorrow? And you'll have to give me her sister's address."

Jon jotted down the address and handed it across the table to Michelle. Her fingertips brushed his as she took it; she glanced quickly at the name of the street, nodding. "Wendall Place. I know where that is."

"It's the third or maybe fourth house on the left—easy to find."

Michelle tucked the address into her purse. After

the waiter had served them small green salads, she said, "It doesn't sound like Mrs. Keaton is ready to face a trial yet."

"Definitely not," he agreed, picking up his salad fork. "I'm going to ask for a postponement to give Dr. Evans more time to work with her to build up her emotional strength."

"That's good, because I'm going to need time with her, too—several sessions before I can testify that she fits the battered woman profile. If I believe she does—"

"I think you'll believe what she tells you. I had to drag answers out of her, but she seemed quite honest to me, and I'm not a gullible man."

"No, you don't seem to be," Michelle said, meeting his green eyes and smiling wryly.

Later, over the veal parmigiana, Jon suddenly put down his fork and openly observed Michelle's face for a long moment. Her features were delicate and finely molded; her skin was translucent and smooth. There was a sparse sprinkling of freckles over the bridge of her small, straight nose. She was pretty, not beautiful; but damn she looked young.

Aware of his stare, she felt uncomfortable. Defensively, she stared right back at him. "What?" she asked rather icily. "Do I have a dab of tomato sauce on the end of my nose or something?"

He chuckled. The sound rumbled up from deep down in his chest as he shook his head. "Nothing like that. I was just noticing again that you look about twenty-two years old."

"I'm older than that."

17

"How much older?"

A puzzled frown nicked her smooth brow. "I'll be twenty-seven next month. Why do you care?"

"It's simple. You look young, and when you're on the witness stand, it may be hard for a jury to believe that you could be an expert at anything."

"Oh, I never thought of that."

He leaned forward in his chair. "Is there anything you could do to make yourself look older for your court appearance?"

"*If* I testify for your client—"

"Okay, if. Is there anything you could do to look older?"

"I suppose I could wear my hair up in a tight bun and wear the glasses I use to drive." Michelle grinned mischievously. "Of course, I could put a paper bag over my head."

"I like the idea about the hair and the glasses," Jon said, grinning back. "But let's rule out the paper bag. Could make a jury a little suspicious."

When lunch had ended, Jon insisted on paying for Michelle's, too. "Expense account," he explained as they walked out of the restaurant. Outside, the sidewalk was crowded with students scurrying around between classes. Lightly gripping Michelle's elbow, Jon guided her through the milling people.

A six-foot-nine member of the university basketball team, paying more attention to the Walkman on his head than to where he was going, nearly stepped on her. She gasped in surprise when Jon's arm slipped around her waist to pull her out of the way. She recovered enough to say, "Thanks. I wouldn't want to be run over by him."

"Big fella like that should be more careful," murmured Jon, his eyes holding hers. "He could squash a little thing like you."

"I'm not that little."

"Compared to someone six foot nine, everyone is little."

"You have a point," she agreed, laughing shakily. She was relieved when his arm left her waist. His abrupt physical action had unnerved her, making her heartbeat quicken and her breath catch. Of course, he had only done it to keep her from being trampled, but still . . .

A minute later, they stopped in front of the door to her office. Michelle extended her hand again. Once again, he shook it, his grip remaining firm a little longer this time. She took a small backward step. He didn't release her hand until she gently extracted it from his and inclined her head. "All right, then. I'll see Doris Keaton tomorrow unless you let me know that's inconvenient for her."

Jon nodded. "Fine. I'll want to know your first impression of her right away."

"Sure, I'll give you a call before five tomorrow. Do you have a business card with your office number on it?"

"Yes, but I'd rather talk to you about Doris in person."

"Okay. Should I come to your Raleigh office, or do you want to come back here?"

"Neither. There's a fine restaurant between here and

Raleigh. Let's have dinner there tomorrow evening and talk."

Michelle hesitated. For an instant she was tempted to accept his invitation. As Debbie had said, he was a very attractive man, intelligent and virile with a good sense of humor and lots of charm. But she shook her head. "I don't think that would be wise, do you?"

"Why wouldn't it be?"

"It's just—it seems to me . . . well, I may end up testifying for your client, and I think we should maintain a strictly professional relationship, don't you?"

"No. Why do you? We may be working closely together for some time, so why shouldn't we become friends?"

"Friendly professionals, yes. But that's as far as it should go, don't you think?"

"Why do you say that?"

Pushing a wavy strand of auburn hair back from her face, she gave him a frustrated look. "Must you answer every question with a question?"

He smiled lazily. "Asking the right questions is my business. And we'll have dinner tomorrow night, okay?"

"I don't think so. Thank you for the invitation, but—"

"Wait," he murmured, swiftly lifting a hand to press his fingertips against her lips, silencing her. His expression altered and became quite serious. "Let me ask you one more thing. Has your work with abused women caused you to shy away from all men?"

"No!" she retorted, irritated that he had come close to the truth. She qualified her answer. "No, not all men, but I have to admit I've become very very cautious about them unless I've known them a long time."

"I can understand that to a certain extent. But loosen up a little, Michelle. I'm only asking you to have dinner."

She had to smile. "I get the message, but I still don't think we—"

"Afraid of me?"

"No, of course not."

"You act like you are."

"Well, I'm not, and okay, we'll have dinner tomorrow evening," she said impulsively, spurred by the challenging note in his voice. Deep inside, she was oddly glad he had persisted. "Just give me the name of the restaurant, and I'll meet you there, say, seven thirty."

"No use us both driving. I'll pick you up about seven. "Just tell me where you live."

He had won the first battle; she was determined to win the second and shook her head. "No, I'd rather meet you at the restaurant at seven thirty."

"Stubborn woman," he called her softly but with a slight smile. "Have it your way. We'll meet at The Gables. Seven thirty."

The moment Michelle entered her outer office, Debbie descended on her. "How was lunch? Is he as great as he seems to be? Did he ask you for a date?"

"Of course not. We talked about his client. I'm seeing her tomorrow and telling him what I think about her tomorrow night at dinner. That's all."

"Oh, dinner. I knew it, I knew it!" Debbie crowed.

"I thought I saw some sparks between the two of you."

"Oh, hush. You're letting your imagination go crazy again," Michelle scolded, walking into her office and closing the door firmly behind her. She went to her desk, put her purse in the bottom drawer, and picked up the file of the woman due at one o'clock. But she closed it again several seconds later and started nibbling a fingernail.

Had there been sparks? Maybe there had—but so what? She was a normal healthy young woman, and he was obviously a normal healthy young man. Maybe there had been a hint of physical attraction, but it didn't mean anything. She saw physically attractive men every day out on the sidewalk, but that didn't mean she was destined to get involved with them.

Picking up the file, she read and forced herself to concentrate.

CHAPTER TWO

The following day, Wednesday, Michelle arrived at the house on Wendall Place at precisely two o'clock. She smiled at the woman in her late forties who answered the door and introduced herself.

"Yes, of course. Mr. Wyatt phoned last night to tell us you'd be here to see Doris," the woman said, opening the door wider to beckon her in. "I'm Doris's sister, Anna Sanders. Oh, I do hope you're going to be able to help her."

"So do I," said Michelle as she stepped into the large, quietly decorated hall. "Before I see Doris, I would like to talk to you for a few minutes, please."

"Naturally. Come into the living room," Mrs. Sanders said, leading the way. "Would you like to have some coffee while we talk?"

"No thanks." Taking a seat on the blue velour sofa, Michelle removed a legal pad from her briefcase. "I'm going to take a few notes, if you don't mind?"

"Not at all. Anything to help Doris," Mrs. Sanders said, sitting down in the matching blue chair across the coffee table. "Poor thing, she's up in her room right now; I'm afraid you're going to have to talk to her there. I can hardly even get her to come down. She just seems to want to hide herself away, even from me. I hope she'll tell you more about her marriage than she's told me."

"Since I'm a stranger, maybe she will," Michelle suggested. "Maybe she feels too close to you to confide. Sometimes it happens that way. You're her older sister, right?"

"Seven years older."

"Jon Wyatt told me you had no idea she was being abused by her husband. Is that right?"

Anna Sanders shook her head, and her expression changed as if the very thought still surprised her. "I didn't have an inkling. Oh, I knew Doris wasn't ecstactically happy, but I imagined that that was because she could never have children and Vincent refused to adopt. He always seemed a charming man to me, although I wasn't at all close to him. Bill—that's my husband—has never cared for Vincent, but he didn't know exactly why. Until now, that is."

Nodding, Michelle jotted down a couple of notes. "Since the shooting, what has Doris told you about her marriage?"

"Very little, as I said. When we were driving her home after bailing her out of jail, I had to ask her why she'd shot Vincent, and she said, 'I thought he was going to kill me this time for sure.' Then she just sort of broke down and sobbed, 'Oh, Anna, he's made me feel so worthless all these years.' I'm still surprised she shot him, though. Doris has always been such a meek person."

"Meek or not, she may have had no choice. She told

Jon Wyatt that Vincent was coming at her with a base-ball bat."

"Oh, my God!" Mrs. Sanders gasped, clapping a hand over her mouth for a second. Stunned, she shook her head. "She didn't even tell me that. God, how vicious of him! Then I'm glad she was able to protect herself with the gun. I can't understand how Vincent could be so violent. Oh, I've seen glimpses of his hot temper from time to time, and he was often impatient with Doris, but to attack her with a baseball bat . . . my God, how horrible. I never would've imagined him capable of that. Of course, as I mentioned, Bill and I didn't really see that much of him. Being a hot-shot writer, he might have thought he was too good for us."

"I see," murmured Michelle as she rose to her feet. "Well, you've been helpful, Mrs. Sanders. Thank you. I may have more questions for you later, but for now, may I see your sister?"

"Sure. Follow me." Anna Sanders led her out of the room into the hall again and up the stairs, where she knocked on the first door to the right.

A pale shadow of a woman answered the knock. On a purely emotional level Michelle's heart immediately went out to Doris Keaton. She looked seven years older than her elder sister, instead of the other way around. Her brown hair seemed faded; her hazel eyes were haunted. Even the expensive designer dress she wore did nothing to make her seem the least bit self-confident.

"Doris, this is Miss Vance," Anna said, "the counselor Mr. Wyatt sent over."

Smiling gently, Michelle stepped forward into the

25

room. "Hello, Mrs. Keaton. May I call you Doris? Please call me Michelle."

"Hello," Doris murmured, the word barely audible.

"Well, I'll leave you two alone to talk," Anna said, starting to close the door. "Doris, sweetie, would you like me to bring up some coffee?"

Doris glanced at Michelle and softly asked, "Would you care for some?"

"No, thank you."

"Then I won't have any either, Anna."

"Okay, honey. I'll go now. You try not to be nervous, and cooperate with Miss—er, Michelle. She's here to help you."

"I know," was Doris's answer, but her uncertain expression belied her words as she turned to face Michelle again. "W-won't you sit down?"

"Good idea. How about over here?" suggested Michelle, leading the way to a small table located in front of one of the wide windows. She sat down in a wicker chair as Doris took the one across from it.

Doris stared at the legal pad Michelle put on the tabletop as if it were a snake coiled to bite her. "Wh-what kind of questions are you going to ask me?"

"Very personal ones," Michelle said honestly. "I'm sorry, but it's necessary."

Doris was the picture of abject misery. "I—I don't know if I can do this. As children, Anna and I were taught to keep our personal lives to ourselves. 'Don't air your dirty linen in public,' our parents always said."

"Yes, but sometimes you have to. This is one of those times. You have to try to open up to me, Doris.

26

You're facing a trial for attempted murder. I may be able to help convince a jury that you shot your husband in self-defense. So you have to be as honest with me about your marriage as possible."

"All right, I'll try." Doris straightened her shoulders a little and seemed to buck up a bit.

Michelle admired her courage in making the effort. "I'm going to be taking some notes just so I don't forget anything you tell me," she explained, then decided it was time to plunge right in. "First thing I need to know: Is your marriage to Vincent Keaton your first?"

Doris winced. "No. I was married before when I was seventeen. Divorced by the time I was nineteen."

"Why were you divorced? Did your first husband abuse you?"

"No. We were just too young. Not really suited for each other. Maybe I didn't try hard enough to make it work."

"Why do you say that? Didn't you try at all?"

"I thought I was trying very hard."

"Then you probably were," Michelle told her firmly but gently. "Do you usually blame yourself when things go wrong?"

Doris almost smiled. "Dr. Evans, my psychiatrist, asked me the same thing. Yes, I guess I do blame myself for a lot of things."

"You shouldn't, but we'll get back to that later. Now, for some easier questions that shouldn't be painful. Tell me about your childhood. Did you have a happy family?"

"Oh yes, I think we were happy," Doris answered,

27

brightening considerably. "Anna and my parents loved me, and I loved them—especially Daddy. I had so much respect for him."

"Was he very strict?"

"Well, in a way. He didn't spank us much—maybe me once or twice—that I remember. Even then he barely swatted my bottom. But he did expect us to be little ladies at all times in our starched dresses, our hair in perfect curls. And we weren't supposed to ever make a fuss. But we didn't have much to make a fuss about. He was so protective of us."

"You had a sheltered childhood, then?"

"Yes, I suppose."

"I see." Making more notes, Michelle went on. "Tell me about your courtship with Vincent."

"Oh, I can't believe it all ended this way!" Doris blurted out, losing her composure and lowering her head. "When we first met, he was such a charmer. He really did sweep me off my feet. I just couldn't resist him, if you know what I mean."

"Yes," Michelle murmured, thinking involuntarily of Jon Wyatt, then pushing that thought far back in her mind, irritated at herself. She returned to the business at hand. "Did Vincent ever hit you before you married him?"

"No. Well, once he almost did. Then he slapped me on our honeymoon, and it got worse and w-worse after . . ." Doris' voice broke, and she began to cry. "I—I can't t-talk anymore right now. P-please don't ask me anything else."

"Okay, no more questions for now," said Michelle, tucking her legal pad and pen into her briefcase. She

28

was unwilling to press the woman further because she was obviously on the very edge of complete nervous collapse. They had made a beginning; there would be other times to learn more about Doris's ill-fated marriage to Vincent Keaton. Quietly she stood, then went around the table to touch the older woman's shoulder. "I won't push you, Doris, I promise. I know this is very difficult for you. But there is something you might do to make it a bit easier. If you could write down the details of the physical and verbal abuse you've suffered, I could take what you write, read it, and then we could talk again. Would that be better for you?"

Stanching the flow of tears with considerable effort, Doris raised her head slightly and nodded. "It could be easier than telling you out loud."

"Then let's try it that way, okay?"

"Okay."

"Write down what you can, and when you have it ready for me, call my office. Here's my card." Taking one from her purse, she put it down on the table. "Or have your sister call me for you."

When Doris only nodded in answer, Michelle slipped silently out of the room and down the stairs. There she was met by Anna Sanders, who thanked her and showed her out.

When Michelle arrived at The Gables at seven thirty that evening, she was informed by the hostess that Jon was already waiting. Escorted to a secluded table, she smiled as he stood to pull out her chair. She couldn't help noticing how handsome he was in gray

29

trousers, light blue shirt, and navy blue crew-neck sweater. He had looked great before in a three-piece suit and tie, and he looked just as great now.

His eyes wandered slowly and appreciatively over her. The powder blue knit dress she wore made her more feminine, clinging in all the right places without being immodest. He smiled his approval. "That dress matches your eyes exactly, Michelle. Very nice."

"Pure coincidence." She laughed. "If you live in Chapel Hill, you have to have at least two or three outfits that match the Carolina blue school color, or they ride you out of town on a rail."

"True." He laughed with her. "Maybe that's why I'm still in the habit of buying mostly blue shirts, even though I live in Raleigh now."

Their light banter was interrupted by a waiter bearing menus. He asked if they would like cocktails.

"I'll have white wine, please," Michelle requested.

"Gin and tonic for me," said Jon.

They looked over the menus silently for nearly a minute before she murmured, "Everything sounds so good; I don't know what to order."

"I can recommend the sole amandine or the shrimp creole. Both are delicious here."

She considered those two choices, then decided. "I'll have the sole."

"Then I'll have the shrimp creole. Halfway through the meal, we can switch plates, and both of us will have the best of two great dishes."

"What a good idea," she said enthusiastically, giving him a pleased grin. "I've never done that before with anybody."

"You don't know what you've been missing. Your germs will be my germs, and my germs will be yours," he quipped, a slow lazy smile gentling his chiseled features. "A sure step toward a closer personal relationship, don't you think?"

"I think you're something of a teaser," she retorted, concealing the rousing effect his words had on her.

After their drinks had been served and the waiter had taken their orders, Jon became more serious. "You did see Doris Keaton today?"

"Yes, I did."

"And? Do you think you might be able to testify for her?"

"From my first impression I think I probably will. But I can't be sure yet until I've had more time with her."

"I understand. But tell me about your first impression."

"Sheltered childhood. Dominant father, which probably made it very hard for her to ever question male authority. She was married once before; it failed, and she seems to feel guilty because it did, although maybe she shouldn't. All in all, she seems to be a very passive woman, easily dominated by men."

"But you don't let someone abuse you just because you're passive. You try to get help."

"Not if you blame yourself for the breakup of your first marriage—and are too ashamed to admit to anyone the second is failing, too." Michelle sighed sadly. "It's all very complicated, Jon. Some girls just aren't taught to stand up for themselves or to respect their own worth. For instance, Doris Keaton and her sister

31

were taught from childhood to be prim and proper always and never to raise a ruckus, to keep their personal problems to themselves. In other words, children —especially girls—should be seen but not heard. It's not an unusual upbringing for battered women who can't seem to put a stop to the abuse until something tragic happens. They don't feel important enough to defend themselves until they finally break. And maybe that's what Doris Keaton finally did—break under the pressure."

"But you're not sure?"

"Not yet."

"Well, you should have plenty of time to make a final evaluation. I'm sure I can get her trial delayed," Jon said. Then he made a dismissive gesture with one hand. "Now let's talk about other things. Doris Keaton's case isn't very cheerful dinner conversation, and we can't be all business all the time. You know what they say—all work and no play—"

"But I didn't tell you that Doris was—"

"Don't tell me now."

"But—"

"Quiet," he murmured, reaching across the table to silence her with fingertips pressed lightly against her lips. "No more shop talk tonight. Might spoil our digestion. Why don't we just get to know each other better? Tell me about yourself."

"Not much to tell."

"Well, you must've been born somewhere and lived somewhere," he said wryly. "Begin there."

"Okay, okay," she acquiesced, laughing softly at his sarcasm. "I was born in Greensboro and lived there until I went off to college. I have one older brother who lives in Dallas now with his wife and two children. My father died six years ago, and my mother remarried last year. I like my new stepfather. He's a very nice man, though he can never take my father's place. Now it's your turn. You must've been born somewhere and lived somewhere," she said with a chuckle, turning his own words back on him. " 'Fess up, Mr. Wyatt."

"I was born in Charlotte and lived there until I came to Chapel Hill to college. I have three sisters. Two older, one younger. My father is retired, and he and my mother do some traveling. Now that we've gone through the basics, we can get more personal. Tell me about your love life."

Michelle stared at him in sheer amazement. "I beg your pardon?"

"Not the specifics," he said with a grin. "I just want to know if you're involved with anyone right now?"

"Oh. No, not anymore."

"Then you were?"

"Yes, about a year ago I was involved with someone, but he turned out to be a different man from what I thought he was."

"How so?"

"My goodness, you're curious!" she said lightly. "Maybe I don't want to talk about him."

"Why? Because he was physically abusive?"

"You're very perceptive. Yes, he slapped me once. I told him to get lost even though he promised it would never happen again. I've heard that story too many times from my clients. They bought it, but I sure didn't."

"That must've been a difficult time for you."

"Oh, I weathered the storm pretty well. Mainly I was relieved that I'd found out about him before I'd gotten more seriously involved. Occasionally I saw him around town, and I hated that. Luckily, I heard he moved away about six months ago. I hardly ever even think about him now."

"No wonder you're sour on men."

"I am not sour on men," she said, laughing softly. "I told you, I'm just cautious."

"Maybe too cautious," Jon said quietly, his gaze holding hers. "I'm not involved with anybody right now, either."

Unsure how to respond to that statement, she was relieved when their waiter arrived with the food.

As they dined on the delicious sole and shrimp creole, their conversation became less personal again. Jon proved to be a very interesting companion: witty, intelligent, knowledgeable on a variety of topics. Michelle enjoyed being with him. Usually she buried her nose in her work and didn't take much time to relax. This evening was a treat—Jon kept her smiling with his amusing comments.

Later, when the waiter offered dessert, Jon looked over at Michelle, unwilling to let the night end so early. He was enjoying her company immensely. "You'll have something, won't you?" he asked. "What would you like?"

"Oh, nothing please. I really couldn't eat another bite."

"At least have coffee, then."

She nodded. "Okay. Coffee would be nice."

"Great. Two coffees, please," he told the waiter, who unfortunately brought it much too quickly to suit Jon.

At last there could be no more delaying the end of the meal. Once again Jon took care of the check, adding a generous tip for the waiter. Then he pulled Michelle's chair as she got up from the table. Together they walked out to the lighted parking lot, and he noticed her shiver slightly. "Cold?"

"A little. The wind's a bit chilly," she answered, gazing for a moment up at the black velvet star-studded sky. "About three weeks till Halloween, so of course it's getting colder."

"Will you be cold driving home? Like to borrow my sweater?"

"Oh no, thank you," she murmured, unreasonably pleased by the kindness of his offer. "I'll be warm once I'm in my car and out of the wind." With one hand she gestured to the right. "I'm parked over there."

"So am I."

They walked on together in silence for a few moments.

"You know what I'm going to do?" Michelle said abruptly. "I'm going to pick up Vincent Keaton's novels and read them. Maybe I can get some insight into his attitude toward women."

"What you find out might be interesting, but I'm afraid it won't help my case even if you decide he's the worst kind of chauvinist. He's not the one going on trial. Doris is."

"I know. I just want to do it for myself—and Doris. Knowing more about him could help me help her open up. She's having a lot of trouble doing that right now." Stopping behind her green Nova, Michelle turned to Jon with a soft smile. "Well, here I am. Thank you for dinner. The food was as good as you said it would be. I enjoyed it."

"I did, too."

"Okay then. I asked Doris to write down specific instances of the abuse she suffered. After I've read them and talked to her again, I'll give you a call."

Reaching out, Jon took her right hand between both of his. "I don't want to wait that long to see you again. We both enjoyed tonight, so let's have dinner again tomorrow evening. No business talk—just for pleasure."

The touch of his slowly stroking fingertips on the back of her hand was exciting, disturbing. Almost trembling, she shook her head. "I don't think so, Jon. We should keep our relationship professional."

"Why?"

She thought fast and hard but couldn't come up with a valid reason. "I don't know why, exactly. To tell you the truth, I make it a rule not to go out with men I haven't known for a long time."

"Rules are made to be broken."

"Not this one. After my experience, I—"

"Forget that," Jon persisted. "Get real. Remember, I have three sisters. I learned to have a healthy respect for females when I was growing up. Hell, I like women. Now here you are, afraid I might try to—"

"I'm not afraid of anything!" she interrupted, flustered enough to yank her hand free of his. "I just don't think it would be good for us to get involved in a personal relationship."

"I think it could be very good for both of us," he murmured, his eyes holding hers. "When we met for the first time yesterday, I felt a chemistry between us. You felt it too. Admit it."

"Well, maybe I did feel something, but—"

He stepped closer, cupped her chin in his right hand, lowered his head, and touched his firm warm lips to hers in an incredibly tender kiss.

Pleasant warmth stole over her. She was too surprised by his quickness to pull away.

After a long moment he stepped back, smiling sensuously. "Did that feel as if I'd ever try to hurt you?"

"Well, no, but—"

"Then how about dinner again tomorrow night?"

She wavered a second, then regained control of herself and shook her head. "No, Jon."

He walked her around the side of her car and opened the door. After she sat down in the driver's seat, he leaned down to look in at her. He tapped the tip of her nose with one fingertip. "Okay, so you're stubborn. But I'm telling you now, I can be stubborn, too. When I want something, I can usually find a way to get it. Right now, I want us to get to know each other better. And I'm going to succeed."

"No, you won't."

"Will too."

"Will not," she retorted, then had to laugh at the childish bantering he had deliberately led her in to.

"Stop this right now and let me shut the door. I'm getting cold, and I want to go home."

Without another word, he shut the car door for her, then stood and watched as she backed up, then drove off the parking lot onto the road. His smile still lingered as he saw her taillights fade in the distance.

CHAPTER THREE

Michelle arrived at home at just past ten o'clock that evening. After parking her car in the driveway beside her tiny rented house, she climbed the three steps to the lighted porch and slipped her key into her front door lock. Before she could go inside, she heard a loud meow. Her cat, Winnie, hopped gracefully down from a shadowed porch railing and sauntered over to twine between her mistress's legs.

"Hello, cat. Guess you're not used to me being out so late, but you can't be hungry. I fed you before I left this evening." Bending down, Michelle scooped her pet up in one arm and carried her into the diminutive living room, where she switched on the light. Winnie squirmed, and she released her. She watched the cat soar down to the polished floor, then stop and lick her paws methodically before giving another, louder meow.

"Oh, stop complaining. You have a great life. You're spoiled rotten."

The fat gray cat obviously didn't agree and meowed gutturally once again.

"You'll just have to wait for me to scratch your

rump," Michelle said as she headed for her bedroom. "First I want to get out of this dress and my pantyhose." She stripped off all her clothes and slipped into her yellow cotton nightgown. Then she put her dress on a hanger in the closet and put her cowhide pumps on the shoe tree on the floor. Winnie shadowed her every step, reminding her mistress she was waiting for her scratching. After Michelle put on her warm fleece robe and stepped into her furry slippers, she picked up the cat again and returned to her living room, where she poured herself a small brandy and switched the television on. Sinking down on the sofa, she propped her feet up on the coffee table while Winnie curled up on her thighs, beginning to purr. She scratched the cat's chin, then her rear end, which made her purr even louder.

The brandy tasted good as she sipped it slowly. And she felt warm in her gown and robe. The house was cool, but not uncomfortably so. She wrinkled her nose when she realized she would have to turn the heat on in only a few weeks. Then the price of heating oil would start eating into her salary again.

The last segment of the magazine-format TV show was ridiculously boring, and Michelle soon shut out the sound. After flexing her paws countless times and digging her needlelike claws into Michelle's robe as she flexed, Winnie had settled down and gone to sleep. Smiling to herself, Michelle stroked the cat's head and allowed herself to think about Jonathan Wyatt. He was a very fascinating man. But possibly dangerous . . .

She must have dozed off for several minutes, because she nearly jumped out of her skin when the phone on the end table next to the sofa rang with a piercing jangle. Her eyes flew open, and she jerked erect so violently that Winnie howled and leaped off her lap to the floor and ran out of the room. Rubbing her eyes with one hand, she ran the fingers of the other through her hair, then picked up the receiver and muttered huskily, " 'Lo."

There was no answer.

"Hello," she repeated, then once again, "hello!"

Still nothing.

"Nitwit, you could at least say you have the wrong number," she grumbled, starting to hang up.

But before she could, a gruff, muffled voice spoke. "Listen up good, Miss Vance. Stay away from Doris Keaton. Stay out of business that doesn't concern you."

Biting back a gasp, Michelle demanded, "Who is this? How did you know I'm seeing Mrs. Keaton?"

"I know. Just remember that and get off the case, or you'll be very, very sorry, lady."

"But—" Michelle winced as the phone at the other end of the line was suddenly slammed down, crashing in her eardrum. For a moment she was too stunned to believe what she had just heard and simply stared at the receiver. Then she began to shake. Never before in her career had she been threatened. Oh, once the husband of one of her clients had come into the office and cursed her profanely for counseling his wife. But she had stood up to him and had obviously intimidated him, because he had retreated like a whipped dog. Most abusive people only prey on those they perceive

41

as weak. And she had shown the man that she wasn't afraid of him.

Tonight was different. She did feel afraid. Jumping up from the couch, she hurried all over the house to be sure all the doors and windows were locked, although she knew very well they were. Breathing deeply, she tried to relax, then went to locate Winnie. She found her crouched under the kitchen table.

"Come out of there, you big silly," she coaxed. But Winnie had a mind of her own, a typical feline trait, and she decided to stay put.

"All right, stay there on the cold floor. I'm going to bed. You could sleep on top of warm covers if you weren't such a ninny."

Michelle did go to bed, but sleep didn't come. After nearly an hour of restless tossing and turning, she sat up with an exasperated sigh. She couldn't forget the threatening phone call; the man's words scared her still. And after only a moment's hesitation, she walked into the living room, called directory assistance in Raleigh, and was greatly relieved when the operator found Jon's home phone number listed and gave it to her.

Jon had just drifted off to sleep when the phone on his bedside table rang. Hoping he was merely dreaming, he let it ring twice more, then sat up with a yawn and an unspoken curse at being disturbed. Yanking up the receiver, he barked into the mouthpiece, "Yeah?"

At the other end of the line, Michelle winced at his tone. "Sounds like I woke you up. I'm sorry, Jon, but I had to tell you what just—"

Jon's tone gentled. "That you, Michelle?"

"Yes. Listen, I got a threatening phone call a while ago from some man who warned me to get off the Doris Keaton case or I would be very sorry."

Jon sat up straighter in bed, frowning. "What did the man sound like?"

"I really don't know how to describe his voice. It was gruff, but I think he was muffling it," Michelle said as she nervously looped the telephone cord around and around her fingers. "The only person I can think of who would threaten me because of my work on this case is Vincent Keaton. But how can he possibly even know I'm involved? He's still in the hospital."

"He might have hired a detective to watch Doris's sister's house. After he saw you there, he might have followed you back to your office to learn who you were," Jon suggested, swinging his legs over the side of the bed to sit on the edge. "That's the only explanation I can come up with. Are you okay, Michelle? Are you very scared?"

"No—well, maybe a little," she confessed. "Mostly shaken up, though."

"Do you want me to come there and stay with you awhile?"

"Oh no, you don't have to do that. I'll be all right soon. I'm already starting to calm down."

"You sure?" he persisted, still very concerned. "I wouldn't mind coming."

"I appreciate your offer, but there's no use dragging you out of the bed. I'm sure I'm safe for tonight. That call was just a first threat. The man, whoever he is, is just giving me something to think about for now."

"I'm sure you're right. Are you thinking about dropping the case?"

"Good heavens, no!" Michelle cried indignantly. "What do you think I am, some kind of coward?"

"Calm down. I didn't mean it that way," Jon answered soothingly. "It's just that you don't receive threats every day, I'm sure, and it certainly wouldn't be cowardly of you to reconsider evaluating Doris. You have every right to think of your own safety."

"Well, as you've told me several times, I'm stubborn. Tonight's threat has just made me more determined to help Doris if I can," she said firmly. "So you think Vincent Keaton is responsible for the threat?"

"Probably. But we couldn't go to the police with any proof. He'd have enough money to cover his tracks. But it may not be him. Could be he has a mistress who wants Doris convicted of attempted murder so she can have a clear field. It's even possible, although unlikely, that one of his devoted readers thinks Doris should go to prison for shooting such a talent."

"There are a lot of crazies in the world."

"Unfortunately, yes."

A sudden thought struck Michelle. "Have you been warned to drop the case too, Jon?"

"Twice. So has Dr. Evans, the psychiatrist. I was going to tell you, but I didn't yet because I honestly didn't think anyone would find out about your involvement this soon. Guess I underestimated whoever's responsible. I'm sorry, Michelle."

"No need to be. I understand," she murmured, not wanting to hang up but thinking she should let him get back to bed. "Well, I won't keep you up any longer. I just thought I should let you know what happened since you brought me in on the case. You can go back to sleep now. 'Night, Jon."

"Wait," he called out quickly, his tone lightening. "Have you changed your mind about having dinner with me tomorrow night?"

"No."

"Come on, break your rule for once. Or at least just pretend you've known me a long time."

"That would be pretty hard to do since I only met you yesterday."

"All right, then. How about this? We've both been threatened by the same person, and that creates a special bond between us that allows us to become closer faster."

Michelle laughed. "You never give up, do you?"

"No. So you might as well say yes."

"All right, then. Yes, we'll have dinner tomorrow night." She finally surrendered, knowing she was beaten. He was a very persuasive man. "But we don't have to go out. I can make dinner for us here."

"Sounds great. What time shall I be there?"

"Seven thirty okay?"

"Fine. Now you have to tell me where you live."

"In a small brick house on the road between Chapel Hill and Carrboro. Closer to Carrboro. There's a huge cedar tree in the front yard, and since it's the smallest house out that way, you can't miss it."

"I'll find you."

His voice had deepened, making his words a promise. Michelle's heart beat faster as she wondered what kind of trouble she might be getting herself into. No trouble whatsoever, she tried to tell herself resolutely with a slight lift of her chin. She could handle Jonathan Wyatt; she certainly could. "Okay," she said lightly. "See you at seven thirty then."

"I'll be there, Micki," he said intimately. "Good night."

She paused, then told him, "No one calls me Micki. I prefer Michelle."

"Oh, but I think there are going to be times for us when I'd rather call you Micki."

She heaved a sigh. "Look, Jon, I invited you here for dinner tomorrow night and that's all. Nothing else."

"We'll see," he teased. He could just imagine that she was blushing right now. "We'll see about that . . . Micki."

Now she realized he was teasing her and sighed again but had to smile. "Oh, you're a real comedian, Mr. Wyatt. A laugh a minute."

"I aim to please."

"Just stop it and go back to bed. Good night." Without waiting for an answer, she hung up the phone with a grin. Then she picked up Winnie and trotted back into the room. "It's late, cat. Time for bed. And tomorrow night you're going to meet a new man. You're a good judge of character most of the time. It'll be interesting to see if you like him or hiss at him the moment he walks in the door."

Winnie didn't even meow. In fact, she acted quite bored at the idea of playing character witness.

* * *

Michelle didn't hear from Doris Keaton on Thursday, but she wasn't surprised. She knew that most abused women find writing about their experiences slow and painful, too, because they are ashamed to admit their relationships with men have failed, usually due to little fault of their own. Michelle knew she would have to be very patient with Doris. And more and more, as she thought about the woman, she felt she fit the battered woman pattern. She wasn't ready to testify to that in court yet, but she was beginning to believe it. Either Doris Keaton was a superb actress, one with Academy Award–winning potential, or she truly had been brutalized by her husband. Michelle strongly suspected the latter.

It was a slow Thursday. Two of Michelle's clients canceled their counseling appointments, but she wasn't worried about them. Both were making good progress, regaining their self-esteem and working hard to make new lives for themselves and their children. One of them had even started dating occasionally, gradually overcoming her fear of men. Michelle was especially proud of her.

During the unexpected free hours, she caught up on some paperwork. When that was finished at about three thirty, she made up a menu for the dinner she would prepare for Jon. She changed her mind about the main dish four times before finally deciding what she would make. By that time, it was after four o'clock. Jon would be at her house at seven thirty. Between now and then, she had to go grocery shopping, drive home, wash her hair, take a bath, dress, then start preparing the meal. Since she didn't have another appointment today, she could leave the office right now and get started on her errands. On impulse, she decided that that was just what she'd do. After getting her purse, she marched out of her office.

"I'm going now," she announced to Debbie. "But you'd better stay until five to lock up in case someone calls. I'll be home by then if there's an emergency."

Debbie stared at her disbelievingly. "Did I hear you right? You're leaving early? My lord, it's incredible! The world's coming to an end. You never, ever leave early. What's going on? Are you sick?"

"No." Michelle smiled. "I just have some things to do."

"Like what?"

"Just things."

"I bet I know," Debbie said with a pleased snicker. "You have a date with that Mr. Wyatt, don't you?"

"It's not a date. I'm having him to my house for dinner."

"Oh, sure."

"Just dinner. That's all I'm giving him."

"Well, I'd be willing to give him more than dinner if he came to my place."

Although unable to suppress a smile at her receptionist, Michelle shook her head admonishingly. "How would your fiancé feel if he could hear you now?"

Debbie grinned. "Oh, he knows I talk big and don't mean half of what I say."

"I'm glad to hear it," said Michelle, opening the door to the street and waving good-bye over her shoulder. "See you tomorrow."

As she walked along the sidewalk toward her parked car, she thought about Debbie's outgoing attitude. She herself was so reserved, sometimes she wished she could let loose a little and be a bit more like Debbie, who was so happy-go-lucky. Maybe it was time for her to become somewhat less serious. Yet she wondered if she could make even that small change.

"You can give it one hell of a try," she said aloud as she opened the door of her car and got in.

By seven o'clock that evening, Michelle had dried her hair, put on light makeup, dressed in gray slacks and a pink knobby knit sweater, and started dinner. Since she had decided to make nothing fancy, she was broiling two rib-eye steaks to be served with salad, baked potatoes, and asparagus tips. A basic meal, one a man would enjoy, she thought as she scurried around her tiny kitchen. Suddenly she stopped dead in her tracks and laughed at herself. She was feeling rather silly, as if she were a teen-ager waiting for her first date to arrive.

"You're not sixteen. You're a woman, so be cool," she muttered aloud, squaring her shoulders and taking a deep breath. All right, so what if Jon Wyatt had managed to upset her equilibrium during the two days she had known him? That didn't mean she had lost control of herself altogether—not at all. So what if he was extremely attractive, intelligent, witty, compelling, and good-looking? That didn't mean she would succumb to all his charms if she remained half as cautious as she had been about men during the past year.

After that mental pep talk, she was able to relax and enjoy preparing dinner. She had always liked to cook, although she certainly was no gourmet chef. In a large wooden bowl she tossed the salad, then covered the bowl with cellophane and placed it in the refrigerator so the greens would stay crisp.

At seven thirty sharp, Jon drove his ivory Jaguar sedan into Michelle's driveway. He was dressed casually in navy trousers, a white shirt, and a light blue sweater. After adjusting his shirt collar, he knocked on the door and waited, a half-smile curving his lips. He was glad he had talked her into having a strictly social dinner with him. There was something very real and strong about her that attracted him. He wasn't exactly sure what it was, but it was definitely there. He was looking forward to spending the evening with her.

A few moments later, Michelle answered his knock and invited him into her small, tidy living room. Sensing a strange presence, Winnie, who had draped herself across a sofa cushion to nap, lifted her gray head and slanted her eyes open to examine the stranger. She didn't hiss.

Looking from Michelle to the cat, Jon smiled and walked over to pet the animal, who arched her back and began to purr as he stroked her.

Behind Jon, Michelle lifted her eyes heavenward. Even her cat seemed to be endorsing him!

Jon glanced back over his shoulder at Michelle. "What's her name?"

"Winston Churchill. Winnie for short. See the resemblance—those fat cheeks? I had to name her after him even though she's a girl."

"I see what you mean about the fat cheeks, but she has more hair than Churchill did."

"Guess you can't have everything."

"Guess not. I think she likes me." Jon smiled lazily at Michelle as her pet nuzzled her chin against his hand. "Do you think that means anything?"

"She's very selective about people," Michelle had to admit, hoping her cat's ability to judge character hadn't slipped on this occasion. She gave him the easiest smile she could manage. "And yes, she does seem to like you."

"I'm glad."

"Please sit down."

He settled comfortably onto the sofa, and Michelle watched bemusedly as Winnie crawled onto his lap and curled up there as if she had known him forever and trusted him completely. "She'll shed on you," she warned.

"I can brush the hair off later."

"Would you care for a drink before dinner?"

"A gin and tonic would be good if you can manage it."

"Coming right up," she said, heading into the kitchen.

When she returned with their drinks a few minutes later, Jon was standing in front of the large bookcase on the left side of the room. "All these titles!" he said, then murmured his thanks when she handed him the gin and tonic. "You obviously like to read."

"Yes, I do."

"So do I, but I don't have much time to."

"Neither do I, I'm sorry to say." Taking a small sip of her brandy, Michelle watched him bend down to pull three paperbacks off the bottom shelf. When she saw what he had, she smiled.

"Aha, romance novels," he murmured, his green eyes teasing. "Now your secret's out. You're a romantic."

She shrugged. "I think most women have romance in their blood."

"Does that mean you think most men don't?"

"Some do, I'm sure. Do you? Are you a romantic?"

"You wouldn't believe how hopelessly romantic I can be at times," he answered softly. "Maybe you'll let me prove it to you tonight."

"Maybe not."

He shook his head in mock dismay. "Had a feeling you were going to say that."

She laughed. It was amazing how easily he could make her laugh, but she wasn't going to let the wondering why disturb her tonight. He had come to dinner, and she planned to enjoy the occasion. She took another swallow of brandy. "I hope you're hungry."

"Starved."

"Good. Dinner will be ready in a few minutes. I'd better go check on it. Would you rather wait in here where it's more comfortable or join me in the kitchen?"

"Lead on. I like kitchens. Besides, I'd be lonely if I stayed in here."

"You'd have Winnie," Michelle said, looking at the cat, who was curled up asleep on the sofa. "She does like you."

"And I like her, too, but I prefer your company. Maybe I can do something to help you."

But there was nothing for him to do. She had every-thing going very smoothly, so he sat down at the table, nursing his drink. He liked watching her efficient, graceful movements as she moved from oven to refrigerator to counter. And she looked good in her gray slacks and pink sweater. Her legs were shapely and long, and her breasts were firm and full against the knit. He also liked the way she flicked her thick auburn hair back over her shoulders when she was concentrating. Yet he wasn't interested in her appearance only. He was interested in the complete woman. He asked, "How was your day?"

"Don't ask."

"That bad, huh? Mine wasn't really a winner, either. What went wrong with yours?"

Turning away from the counter, she leaned back and met his gaze. "One of the women I counsel decided to return to her husband, even though he's never sought help for his problem. She's just going back to what she had before, but she's too afraid to keep trying to make it on her own. It's sad."

"Yes. Your work must depress you sometimes."

"I get down in the dumps once in a while. But I try to see the bright side. I do help most of the women who come to me," Michelle said. "So what went wrong with your day?"

"I was cited for contempt of court and fined twenty-five dollars."

"Why? What'd you do?" she asked, taking the salad out of the refrigerator.

"I sort of overreacted when the judge overruled one of my objections."

"Lawyers have to go to jail for contempt sometimes, don't they?" she asked as she arranged salad on two small plates. "Have you ever been thrown in the slammer for contempt?"

"You've been watching too many Bogart movies," he said with a chuckle. "But yes, I was thrown into the slammer once, for one night."

"What did you do that time?"

"I told a judge he was an idiot," he said with a hint of a grin. "And he was. Luckily, he has since retired from the bench."

Michelle gave him a skeptical look. "You didn't really do that, did you?"

"Scout's honor," he vowed, raising two fingers in a salute. "Of course, that was when I was first starting my law practice. I was something of a hotshot the first year or so, trying to prove myself, I guess. I matured. I don't make personal remarks about judges anymore— at least not in court."

"I should hope not." She walked across the kitchen to peek into the oven. "The steaks are nearly ready. We can start with salad now, or you can have another drink if you like."

Jon shook his head. "One's my limit before dinner."

She served the salads and sat down across the table from him.

After dinner they carried their coffee into the living room. Jon took some encouragement from the fact that Michelle sat at one end of the sofa. He joined her there, although it meant displacing the cat, who protested with a whiny meow when she was moved to a nearby chair.

For several minutes, they didn't talk. But Michelle felt it was a comfortable silence between them. Outside the wind rustled through the heavy boughs of the old cedar tree; one occasionally scratched against the roof. But inside it was warm and cozy.

"Dinner was great," Jon said at last. "And I was really hungry; didn't have much lunch."

"Well, I'm glad you enjoyed it, even if we did have to eat in the kitchen. This house is too small for a dining room."

"At least it's a house. I live in an apartment, and I'm getting tired of it. I've been thinking of buying a house in the country. Do you own this place?"

Michelle almost hooted. "Are you kidding? On my salary I was lucky to afford my car. No, I rent this. More coffee?"

"No thanks."

They watched an old Katharine Hepburn film on TV until a few minutes past eleven. When it ended, Jon reluctantly rose to his feet. "Guess I'd better be going now. Early day tomorrow."

Nodding, she stood, too, then walked him to the door. There he stopped, and she looked up at him.

"Thanks for dinner," he said.

"My pleasure."

He moved quickly to take her in his arms; his fingers slid through her silky hair. He tilted her head back and captured her surprised gasp in his mouth. Hot desire flowed through his veins. With the slowly graduating pressure of his lips, he parted hers.

She had half expected this, but his swiftness caught her off guard. Putting her arms around his waist, she kissed him back, her heart hammering. Thrills rushed over her and trickled down her spine. He smelled spicy; she inhaled the subtle scent of his aftershave. His long, lean body was wonderfully firm and unyielding against hers. But when the tip of his tongue played over her lips and sought entrance to her mouth, the thrill became too intense and jolted her back to good sense. She pulled away from him. "Stop. Enough."

"Not for me," he muttered gruffly, looking down into her lovely blue eyes. "Could I persuade you to let me spend the night with you?"

He wasn't serious, she could tell. She smiled as she shook her head. "No way."

"Damn. I knew that would be your answer, but I had to try," he said, releasing her completely and putting one hand on the front doorknob. "I have to go to Asheville tomorrow for a couple of days, but I'll call when I get back to Raleigh."

"Jon, I don't—"

"I'll call," he reiterated firmly, then leaned down to kiss her again, very tenderly. "Good night, Micki."

Then he was out the door and gone. Michelle closed it after him and leaned back against the wooden panel with a dreamy sigh. *Micki.* She was beginning to like that.

CHAPTER FOUR

The following Sunday morning, Michelle was jarred awake by a loud knocking on her front door. Groggily she slipped out of bed, put on her robe, and walked sluggishly out into the short hall through the living room. She unlocked the door and opened it with a puzzled frown that deepened when she found Jon leaning nonchalantly against the wall of the house. "Wha?" she asked, sleepily rubbing her eyes. "Something happen to Doris?"

"No, no, no. Nothing's happened to anybody," he assured her cheerfully, stepping across the threshold. "I can't believe I woke you up. It's ten o'clock, sleepyhead—time to rise and shine."

"But I like to sleep late on weekends," she murmured, hiding a huge yawn behind one hand. "Only chance I get. Why are you here?"

"I'm here to take you on a picnic."

Becoming more and more alert by the second, she widened her eyes. "A what? Picnic? It's too cold outside."

"Wrong. A warm front moved through here last night. It's going to be an Indian summer day, and

57

we're having a picnic," he insisted, grinning that winning grin of his. "Get dressed, and we'll be on our way. Don't say no—we're going. I won't let you get out of it. I plan to have my way."

Knowing he meant that, she nodded finally. She was inwardly pleased by his surprise visit but was unwilling to show him how pleased she was. "Oh, okay," she pretended to grumble. "But I'm not even half awake yet, so you're going to have to wait. You know where the kitchen is. Please make me some coffee while I shower and dress."

"Hot coffee coming up," he said, smiling as she walked away pulling her robe tighter around her.

In the bathroom Michelle showered, then brushed her teeth and hair. Still yawning occasionally, she applied light makeup. She went into her bedroom and took a pair of jeans and a cream-colored sweater out of her dresser, then shucked off her robe and nightgown. After putting on her bra and panties, she dressed, then stepped into her most comfortable leather espadrilles. Smiling rather bemusedly, she headed for the kitchen.

Jon had just poured himself a cup of coffee. When Michelle walked in, he smiled and poured a cup for her, too. "That didn't take long. And the results are very nice. You look as lovely, as usual."

"Flatterer. I look half asleep, which is what I am," she said, walking over to the table to sit down. He joined her as she took her first cautious sip of hot coffee. "I really shouldn't go with you, Jon. I have lots of paperwork I'd planned to do today."

"That can wait, Micki. You can't work all the time. If you keep it up, you're going to end up as miserable as the women who come to you for counseling, but for a different reason."

"But they need my help so much."

"I understand that, but you can't make them your whole life. Maybe you do it for another reason, too. Maybe you're afraid of having a life of your own, so you hide in your work."

"I do not hide in my work. And I already have a life, thank you. Friends and hobbies," she said crossly. "And if you're going to try to psychoanalyze me on this picnic, let's just forget it."

"Whoa, all right. No more psychoanalysis," he murmured, throwing up his hands. "But don't be so grumpy."

"I'm always grumpy in the morning."

"I'll make a note of that," he said dryly as he glanced over her shoulder. The cat ambled into the kitchen. "We've got company. Winston Churchill, the cat. Where's she been?"

"Oh, she finds a different place to sleep every three or four nights. Once I found her curled up in the bathtub. She just missed having the shower turned on her. She wouldn't have liked that."

"I can imagine." Winnie meowed stridently, demanding breakfast, and Michelle went to get her some food. Jon tried to pet the cat, but the moment he touched her, she arched her back and hissed. Jerking his hand back, he stared at her. "What's the matter with you today? The other night you were friendly."

Michelle grinned at him. "I should have warned you. She's grumpy in the morning, too."

"The two of you together could be dangerous" was his wry response.

Rejoining him at the table, Michelle poured them both second cups of coffee while Winnie crunched her breakfast in the corner. Michelle watched her for a second, then returned her gaze to Jon. "She'll be friendly again as soon as she fills her stomach. I've learned to steer clear of her until she's eaten. And I return to my normal pleasant self after two cups of coffee."

"Then hurry up and drink that one," he pleaded.

She laughed, then asked, "What made you think of going on a picnic?"

"When I saw what a fine day it is, the idea just popped into my head. I like doing things on the spur of the moment."

"Sometimes I wish I could be more spontaneous," she said almost wistfully. "But I usually feel more comfortable when I plan things in advance."

"We're going to start changing that a little today."

"Best of luck. I'm getting old and set in my ways."

"I've noticed you look like you're nearly ready for a retirement home," Jon teased, reaching across the table to lift a strand of her hair. "I see some gray."

"Okay, so maybe I exaggerated." Playfully, she slapped his hand away. "So where are we going for this picnic?"

He adjusted the collar of his red-and-blue-stripe rugby shirt that he wore with faded jeans. "I know a secluded little place by a brook out near the botanical gardens. Very pretty."

"Sounds like you've been there before."

"A few times during my undergraduate days."

"And not alone?"

"Of course not alone. What fun would that have been?"

With a questioning frown, she regarded him carefully. "Are you a womanizer?"

"I like women."

"That's not what I asked you."

"You'd make a pretty damned good lawyer yourself. Great cross-examination skills," he quipped. Then his expression sobered, and he shook his head. "No, I am not a womanizer. And what an old-fashioned word!"

"I am sort of old fashioned, I guess. Raised that way."

"So was I. When I was about sixteen, I think, my dad told me that trying to make a conquest of every attractive woman I met wouldn't be a very fulfilling way to live. I understood what he meant—so no, I'm not a womanizer." He grinned again. "That doesn't mean I promise not to try to seduce you. I couldn't possibly promise that."

"Be still, my heart," she joked, although his words had elicited a quickening sensation in her. Being seduced by him would probably be incredibly exciting. Disturbed by her thoughts, she tried to banish them, but it wasn't easy. She gave him a cautious smile as she played with a tendril of her hair.

He looked at her steadily. "Are you going to eat breakfast?"

"Not this close to lunchtime. I assume you're providing the food for this picnic—or am I supposed to whip up something on short notice?"

"No. I have a basketful of goodies in my car, so if you're ready to go—"

"Just have to get my purse," she said, getting up to head out of the kitchen. She was suddenly eager for this adventure with him to begin. "See you in the living room."

Smiling warmly to himself, Jon watched her go. If she thought he had been kidding about trying to seduce her, she was badly mistaken. There was something about her that really turned him on. Everything about her, in fact.

They met in the living room less than a minute later, but as they started out the front door, Jon stopped short. "Isn't there something you've forgotten?"

She thought hard, then shook her head. "Not that I can think of. What?"

"Your cat, last seen taking a nap behind your stove. Shouldn't you let her out before we leave?"

"No problem. The door to the basement is open, and she's found a secret passageway outside down there." Michelle smiled, remembering. "The first couple times that she used it to get into the house, I thought I was losing my mind. I knew I'd put her out, but suddenly there she was. When she came in the second time, wet from rain, I realized she'd found herself a tunnel in and out of the basement. I went down to take a look, and sure enough, there was a hole in the foundation where the concrete had crumbled—just enough space for her to wiggle through. Now I leave her in the house, knowing she can get out whenever she needs to."

"Smart cat."

"Of course. Would I have rescued a dummy from the pound? I saw how intelligent she was when she trotted out of that awful cage right to me. You could say she picked me more than I picked her."

"Sounds like a dog I had when I was a kid," Jon began.

And as they told each other about pets they'd had in the past, they walked outside into the bright October sunshine. Taking her tinted glasses from her purse, Michelle put them on. "The fall sun's so bright, I'll probably need these."

"I noticed you put them on to watch television," Jon remarked. "You need them for distance, so you must be nearsighted."

"Very." She glanced over at him as they walked away from the porch steps. "Maybe my wearing glasses changes things. Remember the old saying, 'Men don't make passes at girls who wear glasses'?"

Looking at her, he chuckled. "Don't count on it. Your glasses look very fetching on you. They probably even make me more determined to try to seduce you."

Her heart skipped a beat, and she wondered if she was crazy even to think of going on this picnic with him. But she couldn't back out now, she told herself as they walked to his car.

"A Jaguar—how great! Damn, hotshot lawyers must make a lot more money than state employees," she said, eyeing the fine lines of the elegant sedan. "Makes that car of mine look like a heap."

"Glad you're impressed, but don't go overboard. I still have a lot of payments to make on this thing," he quipped, escorting her around to the front passenger side to open her door. "Off we go. It's going to be a great picnic."

As she settled herself, he walked around the car and got in behind the steering wheel. Before he turned the key in the ignition, he gave her a smile. "See, isn't it fun to do something impulsive? I know you've been wondering whether or not you should go with me."

"Not really. I—"

"Yes, you have."

"Well, okay. But I did decide to come."

"And you're going to try to relax and enjoy yourself, aren't you?"

"Will you stop that? You promised not to psychoanalyze me. So just hush and drive," she said lightly. "Please."

"I'm driving, I'm driving," he murmured with a smile as he started the engine.

The site he had chosen for the picnic was as lovely as he'd said it was. After parking the car by the side of a secondary road, they walked a short distance into the woods to a mossy bank of the brook he had mentioned. Gold and red leaves were scattered on the ground, and the bright blue sky could be glimpsed between the boughs of the tall trees.

"It's a nice day and this is a pretty place," Michelle said, looking around. A sparkle of amusement illuminated her eyes. "And very secluded. I can see why you brought girls here. Ever get lucky with any of them?"

Jon grinned at her. "That's a pretty personal question, and I'm not going to answer it. If I say I didn't get lucky, I'll sound like a washout. If I say I did, I'll

sound like a chauvinist pig. So I'm not saying anything."

"Maybe that's wise."

Jon put down the picnic basket and spread out the
blanket he'd taken from the car trunk. When it was
smoothed out, he gestured toward it. "Plop yourself
down."

"My grandmother would be the first to tell you you
don't invite a lady to 'plop herself down.' "

"I do beg your pardon. Here, let me help you sit
down, milady," he said haughtily, despite the smile on
his face. He took her left hand and held it until she
was seated. Then he bowed. "Would your grandmother approve of the way I did that?"

"Yes. She's very big on formalities."

"Doesn't sound a bit like my Grandma Wyatt. She
died about five years ago, but up to the very last minute she was laughing and joking. And that woman
could curse like a sailor."

"No, that doesn't sound like my grandmother. I
said *damn* in front of her once, and she made me sit in
a corner for two hours! I was fifteen years old!"

"Bet you haven't said *damn* in front of her since."

Shaking her head, Michelle chuckled at the memory. "You're right about that. I always watch my language very carefully when I see her. I'm too old to be
told to sit in a corner—I was too old when I was fifteen—but back then she was still able to intimidate
me."

"You don't seem to me like a person who's easily
intimidated," Jon said, joining her on the blanket and
opening the picnic basket. "You're not dropping the

65

Doris Keaton case even though you've been threatened."

"Well, I'm not fifteen anymore. I'm a grown woman with a job to do, and I plan to do it. I got another warning call yesterday, but I can't really take these threats seriously. Can you?"

"They may be idle threats, but be careful, Micki," he warned seriously. "Be safe instead of sorry."

A flicker of fear passed over her face. "Are you saying you're worried about these calls?"

"I'm saying I'm concerned," he explained. "Just don't put yourself in a vulnerable position with strangers. Okay?"

"Don't talk to strangers, huh? Sounds like something my grandmother would say."

"You can talk to them. Just don't trust any of them until after the trial is over."

"A man as well known as Vincent Keaton isn't likely to try to accost me on a public street."

"Yes, but he might hire someone to do his dirty work. By the way, you said you were going to read one of his books. Did you?"

"I bought a copy of one of his novels yesterday and read about half of it last night before I threw it down. I hated it. If that man has any respect at all for women, it doesn't come across in his portrayal of his female characters. They're all dismal human beings for various reasons," Michelle said with a grimace of disgust. "Keaton's writing makes Hemingway read like a women's libber."

"Hm, maybe I'll borrow your copy and read it, too. Could give me more insight into him and help my

66

defense of Doris. Now, enough shop talk. Let's eat," Jon said enthusiastically, taking glossy paper plates decorated with flowers from the hamper, along with plastic forks. He smiled at Michelle and gave a little shrug as he took out paper napkins. "Your grandmother would think I should've brought my best china, silver, and linens, right?"

"Probably, but I'm not as formal as she is, and I think this is very festive."

"You must be hungry by now."

"Famished." Her eyes widened with anticipation as he produced shrimp salad with tomato wedges, cheese, fruit, and crisp brown rolls, along with a bottle of chilled white wine that, he happily noted, was still sufficiently cold.

After he filled her plate with the goodies, she dug in with her plastic fork, enjoying every bite. He did most of the talking while they lunched, and she enjoyed that, too. His voice was pleasant—deep and melodious; his inflection was never monotonous. It was easy to see the effect his voice alone could have on a jury. In everything he said, he sounded so honest. Even his humorous statements rang with a certain wry truth.

"More shrimp salad?" he asked when she had finished what was on her plate. "There's plenty."

"Then I will have a little, please. It's delicious. Did you make it?"

"Sure. Not bad for a bachelor, eh?"

"Not bad at all," she complimented him after a sip of wine. "In fact, it's the best shrimp salad I've ever had. What's your secret?"

"The very light pinch of curry powder I add to my mother's recipe, I think."

"You don't sound too sure."

"Well, I'm not an expert chef. And you're the first person who's ever raved about my shrimp salad. Other people have liked it, but they never called it delicious. Maybe you're just very hungry."

"That isn't it," she insisted. "It really is delicious. I wouldn't lie."

"No, I know you wouldn't," he said with a pleased smile. He thoughtfully tapped a fingertip against his strong jaw. "Maybe I should consider writing a cookbook."

"Maybe so. What are your other specialties?"

"Spaghetti."

The delicate curve of her eyebrows lifted. "That's all?"

"That's about it."

She laughed. "Then you'll write a skimpy cookbook."

He laughed with her. "You're right. It'll be more like a cookbrochure."

The word he concocted struck her as incredibly funny for some reason, and it took her awhile to gain control of her laughter.

He watched her with an indulgent smile until she was finished laughing, then remarked, "It wasn't that funny."

"I know." She nodded, catching her breath. "It just hit me right, I guess. I don't know why. But you do make me laugh a lot every time we're together."

"I'm glad."

"Me too, because you're probably right—I do need to be a little less serious about everything. The work I do can't become my entire life," she said in earnest before starting in on her second helping of shrimp salad.

They finished lunch with fresh fruit. As Michelle sat cross-legged on the blanket, munching a wonderfully juicy and tasty pear, she watched two chipmunks playing at the base of a tree trunk. She pointed them out to Jon. "Whenever I see a chipmunk, I think of Chip and Dale. You know, the cartoon."

"Of course I know," he said, acting insulted. "You happen to be looking at a cartoon lover. My favorite's Bullwinkle."

"Ah, yes. And Rocky, the flying squirrel." Remembering the old TV show, she smiled. "Great stuff."

Jon nodded.

A few minutes later, they went for a walk along the stream, which bubbled and gurgled over the smooth rocks lining its bed. The water was crystal clear; it shimmered in the sunlight that poked through the branches of the trees lining the banks. A turtle sunned itself atop one of the stones protruding above the surface.

Jon took Michelle's hand in his. She made no effort to resist. She felt relaxed, and his lean fingers felt very good slipping between hers. They walked silently most of the time, not needing to indulge in idle small talk to feel comfortable together. It was enough to share the beauty of the woods and the brook. They followed it for nearly fifteen minutes.

Occasionally, Jon glanced over at Michelle and had

to smile tenderly. For the first time since he had met her, she seemed totally at ease with him. He realized her work had to have made her very cautious with all men, but it seemed that she was beginning to trust him. He hoped so, because he was attracted to her more strongly than he'd ever been attracted to any other woman.

At a sharp bend in the stream they decided to go back.

"There's shrimp salad left," he reminded her, squeezing her hand, "if you want it."

"Oh, no. I've had enough. I needed this walk to work off some of the calories."

"You don't have to worry about calories, as slim as you are. You know that."

"Well, thank you for the compliment. And I'm not really worried. But I just feel kind of stuffed. I think I'd rather have a short nap than more food."

"No problem. You'll have a blanket to nap on."

When they returned to the light blue blanket, Michelle dropped to her knees upon it and lay down on her left side, feeling nicely drowsy. Jon had dragged her out of her house before she had properly wakened up, then plied her with food in this beautiful peaceful place. No wonder she felt like taking a snooze.

Lying down beside her, Jon stared up at the clear blue sky through a break in the turning leaves and let her sleep for over a half hour. As the minutes passed and he felt her presence beside him, passion rose in him in heightening waves until he could no longer help himself. He had to touch her.

Michelle awakened when he draped one strong arm

around her waist to pull her onto her back. Startled, her heart started to thud wildly. She moaned softly when he gathered her hair in one hand and lowered his blond head to kiss the side of her neck.

"Jon!" she breathed as rushes of delight scampered over her. "What—what's going—"

"Quiet, my sweet baby," he uttered roughly. Then, taking complete possession of her sweet honeyed lips, he parted them with firm but gentle insistence.

Michelle moaned softly again and slipped her arms around his waist. His muscular upper body pressed her down, and her soft breasts yielded excitingly to the hard contours of his chest. Opening her mouth wider, she moaned once more when the tip of his tongue made delightful contact with hers, toying and stroking, making hot wildfires run all through her, igniting every nerve ending.

"Jon, no."

"Yes, Micki."

"Yes. Yes," she repeated, unable to resist as his fingers played with her hair at the nape of her neck. She no longer wanted to resist; he made her feel wonderfully alive, and his touch was invigorating. And she felt almost faint when his hands cupped her breasts, gently squeezing. "Oh, Jon, yes."

Smiling sensuously, he slipped his hands up under her sweater to the sheer lacy bra that covered her breasts. Her flesh beneath the lace was delightfully warm. Needing desperately to touch it naked, he unclasped the front closure of her bra and slowly peeled the cups aside.

Jon's gentle fingertips floated over her rounded

71

flesh. She gasped, partly from uncertainty but mostly because of the pleasure his touch incited. While his lips, tender yet demanding, played with hers, his hands possessed her breasts. His strong fingers wandered over their softness, probing, toying, teasing. She felt them swell up hotly against his magic touch.

"Oh God, I want you," he groaned. His mouth was at the nape of her neck a moment later as he inhaled the sweet fragrance of her skin. "Micki! I need you. God, you feel so good!"

And he felt good, too—too good. As she ran her hands feverishly over his powerful torso, desire whipped potently through her. Mental bells of alarm jangled in her brain, and she came to her senses. She wriggled away from him to fumble under her sweater and rehook her bra and murmured, "You're going too fast, Jon."

"Damn," he uttered, dropping down onto the blanket on his back, covering his eyes with his right forearm as he fought to control his passion. After several moments, he succeeded and turned onto his side to look at Michelle and smile gently. He nodded his head. "Okay, I was going too fast for you; I understand that now. I hope you won't refuse to see me again because I made this mistake. Will you?"

Perhaps she should have said she would, but she simply couldn't because she realized she very badly wanted to see him again. He was good for her; he made her laugh; he made her temporarily forget her work. And she didn't want to lose that. "I'd be happy to see you again, Jon," she said at last, her voice husky. "But please don't rush me again."

"I'll try not to" was all he could promise as his darkening green eyes wandered slowly over her. "I can only try."

CHAPTER FIVE

About ten o'clock Monday morning, Debbie sauntered into Michelle's private office wearing a big grin. Michelle looked up from her desk. "Need something, Deb?"

"Not really," the receptionist drawled. "I bet you can't guess who I just talked to on the phone."

"You bet right. I have no idea. Who did you just talk to on the phone?"

"Ah, come on! You've got to guess."

"Prince Charles? Oh, I don't know."

"No. Guess again."

"Debbie, please!" Michelle protested, mildly irritated. "I don't have time for guessing games right now. Mrs. Johnson will be here at ten, and I need to review her file before she arrives. So why don't you just tell me who you talked to, if it's so important for me to know?"

"Heck, you're taking all the fun out of it," Debbie muttered, pouting.

"Are you going to tell me or not?"

"Oh, okay." Debbie's face brightened again. "It was *him.*"

Trying to remain patient, Michelle mentally counted to ten. "Deb, *him* could be any man on the face of the earth. Be more specific. Him who?"

"That hunk, Jonathan Wyatt."

"Jon called?" Michelle asked quickly. "Why didn't you put him through to me?"

"He wanted to know if you'd be free to see him sometime today."

"Did you tell him I'd be free at three?"

"No, I told him you were free at lunch."

"Debbie!"

"Well, you will be. But I knew you probably wouldn't tell him that yourself, and I don't think you should miss an opportunity to be with him socially."

Michelle raised her eyes heavenward. "For goodness sake, Deb, I'm capable of handling my own social life."

"But you're not aggressive enough sometimes."

"You mean pushy—like you?" Michelle said wryly. "Your style suits you, and my style suits me. Stop trying to change me."

"But I don't see what's wrong with expecting a man to buy you lunch if he needs to see you," Debbie said with an unabashed grin. "If it were me, I'd order something very expensive."

"I'm sure you would. But enough of this. Am I or am I not having lunch with Jon?"

"You are. He said he'd be here a little before twelve." Debbie smiled suspiciously. "So you're calling him Jon now. How cozy. How's it going with him? Is he a lot of fun to be with?"

"We're working together," Michelle lied—very

75

poorly, she knew, because Debbie giggled disbelievingly. "Okay, yes, he is a lot of fun to be with."

"Details. I need details."

Laughing, Michelle shook her head. "Well, you're not going to get them. I need to skim over Mrs. Johnson's file. And don't I hear your phone ringing?"

"No. I bet you weren't much fun at slumber parties when you were a kid," Debbie grumbled, pouting again. "Don't you know women are supposed to exchange secrets? It's practically written down in the Constitution."

"Is that so? Well, maybe you and I can trade secrets some other time."

"But—"

Chuckling, Michelle pointed her pen at the door. "Out."

"But—"

"Now. Go."

Muttering to herself, Debbie went.

Her client left the office at a quarter till twelve, and Michelle went into the bathroom. She took mascara and lipstick from her purse to freshen her makeup. She was patting translucent powder onto her nose when Debbie popped in the door.

"Oops. Didn't know you were in here." The receptionist smiled knowingly at the compact Michelle had in her left hand. "Touching up the face for Jon, eh?"

"No, for myself. I do this every day before going to lunch."

"Yeah, sure you do."

"Well, most days, anyway."

"Why don't you admit you have the hots for the man?"

"What nice language, Deb!" Michelle said, but she had to grin. "What makes you think I have—as you put it—the hots for Jon?"

"The little light that came into your eyes when I told you he'd called."

"I doubt you saw any little light come into my eyes."

"Yes, I did, and it's still there. Look for yourself."

Involuntarily, Michelle glanced into the wall mirror and discovered that there was indeed some added sparkle in her eyes. But she refused to admit it to Deb. To do so would only invite her to press for details again. She simply shrugged instead. "Hey, do you have to use this bathroom, or did you just come in here to harass me?"

"I need a paper towel to wipe up a little coffee I spilled on my desk." Watching Michelle take a comb from her purse, Debbie promptly took it away from her. "Since I'm here, let me do your hair. Let this wave fall over the corner of your right eye. Men think that's extremely sexy."

"Give me that!" Laughing, Michelle snatched her comb back. "And please get out of here!"

"I know how to take a hint." Pretending to be in a huff, Debbie tossed her head, grabbed a paper towel, and marched out.

Jon arrived at the office at five minutes before twelve. Michelle didn't keep him waiting. When they walked past the reception desk, Debbie called her back, saying there was something she should see before she left.

"What is it?"

"Nothing," Debbie whispered. "I just wanted to tell you he has the hots for you, too. I can tell by the way he looks at you. The two of you make a great-looking couple."

Shaking her head, Michelle walked away without a word.

"Friendly girl, your receptionist," Jon remarked as they stepped outside. Indian summer still prevailed. "I like her."

"I like her very much, too, but she has a vivid imagination. She's sure that you and I are involved in a steamy romance."

"I like her even more now. She has great ideas!"

"I should've known I was feeding you a straight line by telling you about her fantasies," Michelle said, shaking her head admonishingly at him. "Always making with the jokes."

"Not always. As you'll find out," he murmured. He took her arm as he stopped in the middle of the sidewalk. "Where are we going for lunch?"

"We could go back to the same restaurant where we ate before," she said, trying to ignore the warming effect his touch had on her—without success. "Okay with you?"

"More than okay. The veal was delicious."

The restaurant was more crowded today, but they were able to get a table near the center of the room—not an ideal location, but at least not close to the kitchen. After their sodas and salads were served, Jon told her why he needed to talk to her.

"After we have lunch, could you come with me to see Doris?"

Wrinkling her nose, she shook her head. "I'm afraid that's impossible. I have a one-thirty appointment—sort of a group therapy session—and it doesn't help these women's self-esteem if I cancel out on them. I try my best never to do it. But I'm free from three to four." She smiled apologetically. "Debbie didn't tell you that because she thought we should have lunch together."

"What a girl! You'd be wise to keep her. She obviously read my mind when I called this morning because I was going to suggest we have lunch if you didn't have other plans," Jon said with a slow lazy smile. "Your Debbie made it easier for me. Tell her I appreciate that."

"I will not. If I did, her imagination would run wild."

"Maybe it's not her imagination. Maybe she can see into the future as well as read minds," he suggested softly, covering Michelle's hand with his on the tabletop and playing with her fingertips. His gaze held hers. "I think we might soon be involved in a very steamy romance."

She liked being touched by him; perhaps she liked it far too much. That disturbed her. She smiled weakly. "You said you weren't going to rush me."

He released her hand with a nod. "I said I'd try not to. You're right—I just forgot for a moment. Sorry." He got back to business. "Three o'clock is no good for me. I have an appointment back in Raleigh at three fifteen. Could you go after work this evening? I'd like you to come with me because she won't see me alone —I guess all men frighten her right now. She also seems to be reluctant to talk freely in front of her sister. I think she might be more forthcoming if you were with me."

"Probably so. She's ashamed to let someone as close as her sister know how dismal her marriage was. Sure I'll go with you after work. I'd planned to see her today or tomorrow anyway, because she called me this morning to say she had finished writing down some of the episodes of her husband's violence. What time do you want to go?"

"Around six. Should I pick you up at home or at your office?"

"Home. I hadn't planned to work late tonight."

"Good for you. After we've talked to Doris, we can have dinner and maybe go dancing."

She sighed. "You said you weren't going to rush me."

"How am I rushing you by asking you to have dinner and go dancing? How dangerous could I possibly be in a restaurant or on a dance floor?"

"Not very, I suppose," she conceded with a little smile. "Okay, we'll have dinner—maybe even go dancing. I haven't been out dancing for a long time, so I might step on your toes."

"I'll survive," he said dryly, picking up his salad fork.

80

* * *

Doris Keaton was making progress in rebuilding her confidence and self-respect. She summoned up enough courage to leave her bedroom and met with Michelle and Jon in her brother-in-law's study. Once again she was dressed in an expensive designer outfit—this time, a beautifully tailored rust suit—and although she mainly kept her eyes downcast, there was more life in them. Jon noticed that she seemed less afraid of him as he and Michelle sat down on a tan leather sofa that faced the matching chair where Doris sat.

Trying to smile, Doris leaned forward and handed Michelle two sheets of paper that she had been holding on her lap. "I wrote about some of the times, describing what he did to me. Not nearly all—that would take months to put down on paper. But the times were pretty much the same. You know, he'd either hit me a lot or scream at me about what a nothing I was."

"Let me read this quickly, then I'll have some questions to ask," Michelle told her.

As Michelle read, Jon engaged Doris in small talk, hoping to make her more relaxed. He had a question for her, too, but decided to wait until Michelle had asked her own.

Nibbling her lower lip, Michelle read an account of the physical brutality and mental cruelty typical in the lives of most abused women. She no longer had any doubts that Doris Keaton had been tormented for years by her husband. Now she knew she could testify to that in court in good conscience. After finishing the second page, she looked up at Doris with compassion in her eyes.

"You wrote that whenever your husband beat you, he hit you in the abdomen or ribs so the bruises wouldn't show."

"Yes, he didn't want anyone asking about bruises. He knew that if no one asked how I got hurt, I'd never tell anyone how he treated me." Doris flinched at the memories. "And he was right. I couldn't tell anyone until it was too late."

Michelle nodded, her expression sympathetic. "I get the impression from what you wrote that his verbal abuse was almost as bad as the beatings he gave you. True?"

"Maybe so. I mean, I couldn't do *anything* to please him. He demanded that I entertain his friends, and I tried hard to be a wonderful hostess. But even after very successful parties, he would yell at me and tell me I'd done everything wrong and that he was ashamed to be my husband." Doris sobbed once, then recovered her composure. "He gave me money and told me to buy some decent clothes. I bought the most expensive fashionable things I could find, but he still told me I was a mess, that I looked like an old hag. Nothing I did ever pleased him. Nothing. Nothing, and I tried so hard. But the worst thing . . ."

Her words faltered. "Tell us," Jon gently prompted.

"I can't have children. I've always wanted to have a baby, but about ten years ago several doctors told me it would be impossible for me to conceive. Vincent never even wanted a child—he hates kids—but that didn't stop him from screaming at me that I was only half a woman because I couldn't even give him a baby. He seemed to hate me so and seemed to want to destroy me. If I get sent to prison, I guess he succeeded. Now I wonder more and more why I let him do those things to me all those years."

"Did you ever ask him for a divorce?" Jon asked.

"Several times. He refused. Said he wasn't going to give me half of his assets, because I hadn't earned them, because I was a total bust as a wife. I think maybe he was hoping to push me into killing myself. That thought crossed my mind many times, believe me.".

Michelle proceeded delicately. "This is going to be an uncomfortable question for you to answer. Up until the night you shot your husband, you'd never done much to defend yourself. Why was that night different?"

Doris shuddered. "His eyes; they were different somehow. The anger in them was colder, meaner. I could see that he meant to take that bat, and . . . he wanted to kill me. I could see it. I panicked completely, grabbed the gun, and pulled the trigger. It was the look in his eyes—that look."

Without thinking, Michelle reached over and squeezed Jon's left hand. She smiled beamingly at Doris. "You've just given me the typical abused woman's answer—at least the ones finally forced to defend themselves. The man's eyes change, show some kind of intent to kill. Oh, I think we're going to do great in court."

"Don't count your chickens before they hatch," Jon warned. "We're going to need more than that to convince a jury that you acted in self-defense. I have a very important question to ask you. Are there any witnesses who could testify that Vincent is capable of violence?"

"He was always charming around other people. He could put on a great act most of the time, but—"

"But what?"

"Well, he used to play softball with some of the neighborhood men. I used to go to the games until a couple of years ago, when he told me he didn't want me there anymore because he was ashamed of the way I looked. But at one of the last games I went to, Vincent struck out. He just exploded, started to attack the umpire until his teammates held him back. I can give you the names of some of the men on the team, if that would help."

"It would, very much."

Doris went to her brother-in-law's desk for a slip of paper and a pen. While she wrote down the names of Vincent's teammates, Michelle and Jon talked quietly. When Doris finished, she handed the list to Jon, who glanced at it, then put it in his briefcase. "I'll certainly interview these men. Now, Doris, there's another question I don't like to ask but have to. You know that Vincent is telling the DA that you were waiting with the gun to ambush him the night he was shot so you could inherit all his money and marry the other man you were seeing. Please tell me the truth. If there was another man—"

"Another man! You must be joking. Vincent's behavior has made me afraid of all men. I even feel uneasy around my brother-in-law, even though he's the kindest man I've ever known. No, I was not having an affair."

"What about Vincent? Did he run around with other women?"

"I think he has a mistress. I don't know who it is, and I can't even prove she exists, but there were many times when I didn't know where Vincent was. Toward the end, I didn't much care where he was or who he was with. He was treating me so horribly, I was just glad when he wasn't home."

"My investigator may be able to learn who he was seeing, if anyone," Jon said, looking at Michelle. "That's all I have to ask Doris tonight. If you don't have any more questions, we can go."

"No. I'm finished, too." Standing, as did he, Michelle smiled at Doris. "I hope writing down some of the things Vincent did to you helped you begin understanding your feelings."

"It did a little. Now I'm finally beginning to wonder why I let him treat me so badly for so many years."

"He stripped you of all your self-respect, which was what he intended to do. And he blamed you for everything so much, you started blaming yourself. Typical. Doris, I have a therapy group you should join. You could talk about your experiences and share your—"

"No!" Doris said quickly, her eyes widening in fear. "I couldn't do that."

"I wish you would join the group sometime before the trial," Jon suggested. "You need to get used to talking about your marriage before I put you on the stand."

"And these are women who know what it was like for you, because they've all been through the same hell," Michelle added. "Do think about joining."

85

"I know I can't now. Maybe later."

"I strongly urge you to join," Jon persisted, then left it at that, not wanting to push the nerve-wracked woman too far.

As they started out of the study, Doris fell in beside Michelle. "Bill tells me Mr. Wyatt is one of the best lawyers in the state," she whispered so that only Michelle could hear. "But he's a nice man, too, isn't he?"

"First class," Michelle whispered back. "And you don't have to be afraid of him."

"That's easy for you to say."

"You'll start to feel less and less scared as time goes by," Michelle reassured her. "You'll see."

"I hope you're right."

"Who's the expert, you or me?"

"You are," Doris said, actually laughing a little as she walked them to the front door.

Back in the car a few moments later, Michelle looked somberly at Jon as he started the engine and began backing out of the driveway. "What are her chances of being convicted and sentenced to prison?"

"Right now, I'd say we have a fifty-fifty chance of winning an acquittal. It's her story against Vincent's, unless I can get witnesses who can testify that he's a violent man."

"Then you've got to find some. God, we have to help that woman."

Turning onto the street, Jon glanced over at her. "Then you've decided you can definitely testify on her behalf?"

"I did tonight. When I read what she had written,

86

then when she told me that his eyes changed when he came after her with the bat, I lost all my doubts."

"Good. Didn't I tell you the first time we met that she would convince you she was telling the truth?"

Michelle gave him a grin. "Yes, you did, but don't gloat about being right."

"Why not? I'm usually right. I know I was right about you,"_he said, his deep voice softening. "I knew you could relax and have fun if you'd just let yourself. And we're going to have fun tonight. I made reservations for us at the Pallidin Room."

She raised her eyebrows. "What'd you do, rob a bank? That place is outrageously expensive."

"You only live once."

"Go to the Pallidin Room often enough, and you'll have to start living in the poorhouse."

Reaching over, he tugged a strand of her hair. "Don't be such a worrier. If I couldn't afford to take you to the Pallidin Room, we wouldn't go."

Michelle ran her hands over her moss green suit. "I'm not really dressed for such a fancy place."

"So we'll carry our briefcases in and act like two busy young executives who've just come from the office."

"Well, okay. Just don't compare me with the other women, who'll be in jewels and slinky dresses."

"I wouldn't think of it. You're incomparable, anyway."

"And you're a smooth talker, Jonathan Wyatt."

He smiled at her. "We lawyers have to learn to be slick."

Twenty minutes later, the maître d' in the Pallidin

87

Room glided across the floor, leading them to a cozy table for two beside a potted palm. In silky tones, he wished them an enjoyable evening, then glided away again. As they were putting their briefcases under the table, a waiter arrived with menus, and they ordered drinks. Michelle had white wine, and Jon ordered a gin and tonic. As Michelle opened her gilt-edged menu, her eyes went wide.

"Good Lord, will you look at this?" she whispered across the table. "The prices are so high, they don't even put them on the menu. You're going to have to skip this month's car payment just to pay for dinner."

"I'll be able to make the payment, and I told you not to worry," he said firmly. "Just look at the menu and decide what you want."

Her eyes skimmed the page. "I'm sure Debbie would advise me to order the most expensive item, but I don't care for lobster."

"Neither do I. You see, that's one more thing in common. We're practically made for each other, woman."

Aroused by his words, whether he truly meant them or not, Michelle tried to remain calm and cool. "This sounds good: broiled perch with cucumber sauce, served with steamed zucchini and tender new potatoes. I think I'll have that and a small salad."

"Sounds good to me. I'll have that, too," said Jon, ordering for both of them when the waiter returned with their drinks.

The meal started well. Their salads—Belgian endive and watercress topped with bleu cheese dressing—

were delicious. Soon after they finished them, the entrées were served.

Michelle moaned ecstatically after her first bite of fish. "Oh, how delicious! Of course, it should be. This is going to cost you an arm and a leg."

Jon glowered at her, his jaw tightening. "If you say one more word about the prices in this place, I'm going to take you in my arms in front of all these other people and kiss you until you shut up," he warned. "Now, wouldn't that embarrass you?"

"Yes," she answered, laughing, knowing he was only bluffing. Or was he? Suddenly she couldn't be sure, and she vowed, "I won't say another thing about it, I swear."

"Good," he murmured, his expression amused.

After they finished dinner, Jon led Michelle out onto the dance floor. A small band was playing a waltz. Smiling, they went slowly into each other's arms and began to move to the slow, sensuous beat. As Jon's arms tightened around her and his large hands rested lightly on her hips, Michelle laid her head in the hollow of his right shoulder and closed her eyes. The next tune the band played was another waltz, and they continued to sway together amid the other dancing couples. Michelle felt right at home in his embrace; their bodies seemed to fit together like matching pieces of a puzzle.

"I hope they keep on with slow music," Jon whispered huskily into her ear, his warm breath stirring her hair. "If they change to something fast, you're liable to be trampled by my big feet."

"I doubt that," she murmured. "You're a good dancer."

"Only when the music's slow. When it gets fast, I become a klutz and a physical danger to anyone around me. Self-consciousness, I guess."

"You? Self-conscious? I don't believe it."

"That's because you don't know what I was like in high school. I was known as something of a nerd. I did play football, but my claim to fame in that sport was my record number of fumbles in one season—a record that still stands at my old alma mater, as a matter of fact." He nuzzled her earlobe with his lips before adding, "I hope you realize I'm trusting you with a secret I hope never gets out."

"I'll never tell," she promised softly, trembling a little as his breath tickled her neck. "I had some bad moments in high school, too. I was looking through my old diary the other night, and it seems I spent the entire tenth grade hoping my face would clear up and wishing I had a boy friend. I can't really remember now, but it must have been a miserable year for me."

He chuckled. "Being a teen-ager's not all it's cracked up to be. Our parents ask why we're not happy and tell us, 'These are the best years of your life.' But I sure wouldn't want to relive them."

"Oh, neither would I."

They danced for another couple of minutes. Then the band quickened the tempo, and Jon pulled away with a comical grimace. "That's it for now, unless you want to witness utter carnage as I stumble over everybody and everything."

"No, I wouldn't want that," she said, laughing as he escorted her back to their table.

They left the Pallidin Room at ten thirty after dancing to all the slow numbers the band played. Outside, the air had become cooler. Michelle wrapped her suit jacket more tightly around her as they exited the parking lot.

Back at her house, Jon got out of the Jaguar to open her door and walk her up the porch steps. Swiftly, mentally, she debated whether she should ask him in, then decided it wouldn't be wise to do so. Dancing with him had aroused her to the point of feeling vulnerable. Yet she hated for the evening to end so soon.

"Thank you for dinner," she told him in the soft porch light. "It was delicious, even if it must've cost you—"

"I told you not to say another word about that," he muttered, silencing her with a gentle hand to her mouth. "And I told you what I'd do if you did."

"Yes, but now there's nobody around, so I wouldn't be embarrassed if you made good your threat."

His fascinating green eyes narrowed. "Is that an invitation, Micki?"

Smiling slightly, she nodded. "Yes, I guess it is."

"I accept." Taking her into his arms, he covered her warm, soft lips with his.

She pressed against him for several delicious moments, then drew back. "Jon, I'd better go inside."

"Come on, you have to ask me in and offer me a brandy at least," he cajoled teasingly. "After all, it's getting colder out here by the minute, and I need something to keep me warm for the drive home."

He was persuasive. She nodded at last. "Okay, one brandy coming up."

Inside the house, she left him in the living room and went into the kitchen to pour two brandies. When she returned carrying two half-full glasses, she found him lighting the kindling in the grate of the fireplace. She stopped short in the doorway. "What—"

"It felt chilly in here to me," he said with great aplomb. "Thought a fire would be nice. And since you already had the wood arranged in the grate, I started one."

As flames licked through first the dry kindling and then the larger logs, Michelle had to smile. An instant sense of coziness filled the room. She didn't protest when Jon tossed throw pillows from the sofa onto the area rug before the fireplace. He stretched out before the fire, resting on one elbow; she lowered herself down beside him, handing him his brandy.

His eyes holding hers, he took it from her and asked, "Where's that cat of yours?"

"Oh, she likes to roam around at night."

"Aren't you afraid she'll wander onto the road and get hit by a car?"

"No, she's very bright. Always has stayed away from the road. And there are woods behind the house where she goes to harass rabbits and squirrels—anything she can find. She's quite a menace to the wildlife around here."

Smiling sensuously, wanting to hold her close, Jon took her glass of brandy from her hand and placed it next to his on the brick hearth. Moving closer, he slipped one arm around her waist and drew her toward him as he said gruffly, "Come here, honey."

Her breath caught. Her heartbeat went wild, and she went to him eagerly, despite all the reservations in the back of her mind. For once, she allowed her heart to rule her head.

CHAPTER SIX

"Let's get more comfortable," he said, pushing her jacket off her shoulders. While she shrugged out of it completely, he removed his own, along with his tie. Michelle watched with rising excitement as he opened his collar. He smiled. "That's better, isn't it?"

"Yes," she murmured, pleased when he laid one hand on her hair.

"You don't have the hot temper redheads are supposed to have," he said softly, running his fingers through silken strands. "Or have you just been keeping it hidden?"

"That's a myth," she told him, her scalp tingling at the touch of his grazing fingertips. "I'm sure most redheads have fairly normal tempers."

"Underneath that surface reserve of yours, I have a feeling passions run strong. Why don't I find out?"

"Jon, I—"

He kissed her very tenderly at first, then with a slowly increasing pressure that parted her lips. Wild sensations scampered over her, and she moved closer to him, basking in the warmth of his strong arms tightening around her. Her hands glided over his broad shoulders to clasp together over the nape of his neck.

Settling her down with him on the cushions, Jon held her closer still. Her body was soft and warm against his, making him feel he could never get close enough. They kissed again and again. Her ardent response intensified the searing desire running through his bloodstream.

"You taste like honey," he murmured between kisses. "Good, so good, Micki."

"You . . . taste good, too," she admitted, her heart fluttering as his lips nuzzled and played with hers. Closing her eyes, she sighed softly. His hands moved around from her back to cup the rounded sides of her breasts. Pulling away slightly, he began unbuttoning her white silk blouse. Maybe she should have stopped him then, but she didn't want to. He was making her feel too good.

When the buttons were undone, he opened her blouse, and his eyes darkened as he looked at her. She was wearing only a thin lacy bra and a half slip beneath her skirt. With one fingertip, he caressed the swells of feminine flesh rising above the cups of her bra, smiling faintly when she moaned with obvious pleasure. Encouraged, he unfastened the front closure of the bra.

"I've touched you here before, and I'm going to touch you again now," he told her huskily. "But this time I have to see you."

Her eyelids fluttered open, and she was thrilled by the look in his eyes as they slowly roamed over her upper body. The quickly deepening passion evident in their emerald depths was tempered by incredible tenderness, which strengthened her ever-growing regard for him. His gaze traveled up to meet hers, and he smiled faintly.

"You're beautiful, Micki."

"You're making me feel beautiful," she whispered. "And I like it."

"Honey," he whispered back, watching her face as she lifted her hands to his shirtfront and started undoing his buttons. Then as her smooth slender fingers drew erotic designs over his bare chest, he groaned and lost control for an instant. Swiftly, he turned her onto her back on the cushions, knelt beside her, and bent down to kiss the taut underslopes of her breasts. His thumbs played with her nipples, causing them to harden to erect nubbles of aroused flesh.

Michelle felt light-headed in the heat and raw emotion that he was creating deep inside her. Sweeping her arms around him, she moved her hands up and down his powerful back beneath his shirt. Finally she unbuttoned his cuffs with slightly shaky fingers and uttered breathlessly, "Let me help you take that off."

"My pleasure." Straightening a bit, he allowed her to remove his shirt. Then he was encouraged when her hands curved over his shoulders and urged him back to her. With his hands and gently probing fingers, with his lips, tongue, and teeth, he explored the soft glory of her breasts, taking each of the twin peaks in its turn into his mouth.

On fire, she lightly raked her nails down his spine as wanton sensations swirled in her, gathering centrally in an empty aching. She wanted him to go on touching her forever, but when he slipped a hand beneath her skirt and moved it slowly upward, she realized she had allowed things to go too far for her own peace of mind.

She had become very fond of Jon but had no idea how he really felt about her. If they made love, she would be making a personal commitment. But would he? She simply didn't know. Yet she wanted him completely. The rational part of her brain battled with her physical need. At last rationality won out. With reluctance, she stilled his hand on its upward journey over her thigh.

"I'm not ready for this. I don't want to seem like a tease," she murmured regretfully, "but I'm just not ready, Jon."

He groaned softly. "Micki, you can't say no now."

"I . . . have to. Try to understand."

He took a deep breath. He knew when to give up, and finally he nodded. "I'll try. But I think I'd better get away from you before I change my mind about that. Unless it's at all possible that I might be able to change yours?"

Smiling slightly, she shook her head.

Ruefully, he smiled back, then put on his shirt, tucked it into his pants, and put on his jacket, while she rehooked her bra and slipped back into her blouse. She walked him to the front door, and he paused for a moment. "I don't think you're a tease, Micki, but you do owe me something for making this a rather frustrating night. So I insist you have dinner with me in my apartment tomorrow evening."

She was tempted—oh, so tempted—but she needed time to think and told him that.

"Think about what?"

"Where our relationship might be heading."

"Sometimes it's wiser to go with your feelings," he said seriously, taking her chin gently between a thumb and forefinger and tilting her face up. "Sometimes you can think too much."

"But you know I'm a very cautious person."

"Indeed I do," he answered wryly, but he didn't entirely give up. "All right. You do your thinking after I'm gone. I'll give you a call tomorrow afternoon to see if you've changed your mind about dinner at my place."

"But Jon, I—"

"Talk to you tomorrow," he cut in, and leaned down to give her a quick but passionate kiss on the lips. Then he opened the door and abruptly left.

After he was gone, she felt more than a little confused.

After Michelle arrived at her office Tuesday morning, the day rapidly deteriorated. Debbie was already there and sat grumbling at her desk. Michelle gave her a puzzled look. "What's the matter with you?"

"Oh, the phones are out—dead as a doornail."

"Wonderful. That's just great. Have you called the repair department at the telephone company?"

"No, I thought I'd better wait for you to get here to hold down the fort."

"Well, go next door to the bookstore right now and call them. Tell whoever you talk to that we provide a public service and sometimes get emergency calls from women who need our help immediately."

Nodding, Debbie hurried out. Ten minutes later she returned, wearing a harried expression. "I got put on hold three times and talked to four different people, finally a supervisor. I think I convinced her we have to have working phones. Anyhow, she promised that our problem will be given top priority. She said a repairman would be here within an hour. We'll see about that."

"All we can do is hope," Michelle said from her desk. "Now, let's get to work. Do you have Mrs. Winston's file? I can't find it in the cabinet."

Frowning, Debbie went into the outer office. She returned less than half a minute later with the supposedly missing file. "It was right where it should be. You just missed seeing it. Why? Love getting in your eyes?"

"Don't start that again. You're being ridiculous."

"Oh, am I?"

"Yes," Michelle said, but she knew she might be lying. Maybe she *was* beginning to fall in love with Jon. That thought frightened her. She glared at Debbie for putting the idea in her head. "Try to curb that outrageous imagination of yours and get to work. We have a full schedule today."

Shrugging but smiling knowingly, Debbie went back to her own desk.

Less than twenty minutes later, Michelle heard her receptionist's startled shriek coming from the tiny storage room at the back of the building. Michelle raced to the door but stopped short just past the threshold. Her eyes darted around the walls; they were covered with obscene words and graffiti. Garbage was strewn over the floor.

"I came out here for a box of typing paper, and this is what I found," Debbie said, shaking her head disbelievingly. "Who would do this kind of thing?"

"I think I might know," Michelle murmured, suddenly suspicious of the lack of telephone service. "I just think I might."

"What do you mean?" Debbie questioned, but there was no time for Michelle to answer because the telephone repairman joined them that moment, curiously looking at the obscenities scrawled over the walls.

"Looks like you've had vandals here," he drawled laconically. "Think it has anything to do with your dead phones?"

"Could be, but I can't be sure until you find out what's wrong with our lines." Michelle followed him out back into the small alleyway, where he soon discovered the problem. "Looks like somebody deliberately cut your line, miss," he told Michelle as Debbie hovered in the doorway. "I'll splice them back together and restore your service."

"Thank you very much," Michelle said, going back inside prepared for questions from Debbie.

And she got them.

"What's going on? Who would want to cut our phone lines? Do you know what's happening?" the receptionist asked in rapid fire. "There's something you're not telling me. What is it?"

"I've been warned to drop the Doris Keaton case. I told you about her—the woman who was finally forced into defending herself. She shot her husband and is being tried for attempted murder. Jon Wyatt's client."

"I remember. What do you mean, you've been warned to drop her case?"

"Well, I've sort of been threatened that I'd be sorry if I didn't drop it."

Debbie was horrified. "Why didn't you tell me what was going on?"

Michelle smiled wryly. "Because even though you're younger than I am, you try to mother me, and I didn't want to worry you."

"Thanks a lot," Debbie uttered, truly put out as she marched back into her own domain, the outer office.

A few minutes after Michelle returned from lunch, Debbie entered her office, her face pale, her lips trembling. Seeing how distraught the younger woman was, Michelle rose from her desk and went to her immediately, clasping her shoulders. "What's the matter?"

Debbie gulped several times, then gasped, "I just got a call. Some awful man with a raspy voice told me to convince you to drop Doris Keaton as a client or both of us would be very sorry."

"Damn, damn, damn. I never figured they would lean on you, too," Michelle said, then smiled wanly, understandingly. "Listen, if you'd like to take a leave of absence until the Keaton trial is over, I'll approve your request for it. I don't want you to be in any danger just because I'm too stubborn to give up on a client. Just say the word."

"No way," Debbie stated firmly, visibly bucking up. "I love my job. It's important—you and I help women who are desperate. No bully on the phone is going to make me run away from something that important."

"You're very brave," Michelle told her, proud of the

girl's courage. "But I want you to be careful every minute of the day."

"I will. I'll have my fiancé spend every night with me. He can drive me to work in the morning and pick me up in the evening."

"Good idea. Right now you'd better call the police and report the vandalism, even though there's not much chance they'll find out who's responsible for it."

Nodding, Debbie went away, and Michelle went to her desk to call Jon. This vandalism thing was the last straw as far as she was concerned. Surely there must be some way to prove Vincent Keaton was behind the harassment. After dialing Jon's office number, Michelle heard it ring twice before his secretary promptly answered.

"This is Michelle Vance calling. May I speak to Mr. Wyatt?"

"I'm sorry, Ms. Vance, but he's in a meeting at the moment. Would you like to leave a message?"

"Yes, please. Tell him I need him to call me back as soon as possible. It's very important."

"Is it urgent?"

"I think so."

"I see. Then hold a second. I'll buzz him and ask if he can speak to you for a moment right now."

"Thank you," Michelle murmured, then waited. Seconds later, Jon came on the line.

"Micki, what is it?"

"I'm sorry to disturb your meeting, but I thought you should know we've had trouble at my office. This morning when we came in, we didn't have phone service. The repairman thought the wires had been cut.

102

We discovered the back room had been vandalized when he went to check our lines. I imagine someone broke in here last night," she told him and sighed. "Don't you think things are going a little too far, Jon? Debbie just got a threatening call from a man who warned her to convince me to drop the Keaton case. That's outrageous!"

"It's been outrageous from the beginning," Jon said tersely. "Did you call the police about the vandalism?"

"Debbie's just doing that. We should have called right after we saw the back room, but I was so upset, it didn't even cross my mind. Jon, isn't there a way to link Vincent Keaton to all of this?"

"I have my investigator working on it, but he's come up empty so far. I'm sure Keaton's covering his tracks very well," Jon said rapidly. "Listen, Micki, we need to talk more about this, but I have to go right now. I'm in a meeting. Guess you'll have to have dinner at my place tonight after all. The address is on my card. See you at seven. 'Bye."

Without waiting for her to say anything, he hung up, leaving her sitting at her desk with a blank look on her face. For several moments she continued to hold the receiver to her ear but finally replaced it in its cradle.

"The nerve that man has!" she grumbled aloud, shaking her head. "Dinner at his place, my foot! I'm not going." She smiled to herself then, knowing she would.

Debbie stuck her head in the door. "Did you say something to me just a second ago?"

Michelle waved a dismissive hand. "No, no, just talking to myself."

"Getting senile already?"

"I think I still have a few years to go for that. Did you reach the police, Deb?"

"Yes. They're sending an officer right over."

"Good. Send him in here when he arrives."

He turned out to be a she. Officer Marie Austin entered Michelle's office about five minutes later. A sturdy young woman of medium height, she had a very pretty face but a no-nonsense look in her eyes. Escorting her to the back room to see the damage, Michelle had a feeling Officer Austin would have trouble protecting herself or anyone who needed help. Not wanting to waste her valuable on-duty time, she quickly explained about the cut phone lines, motioned toward the scrawled words on the wall, and then told her about the threats both she and Debbie had received.

"You say your receptionist has been threatened once. How about you? More than that?"

"Yes."

"Always here at the office?"

"No, always at my home, as a matter of fact."

"And you're warned to drop one of the women you're counseling? What's her name?"

"Doris Keaton."

Officer Marie Austin frowned. "She's the one who shot her husband, right?"

"Yes, she did, in self-defense."

"Claimed he was after her with a bat. Yeah, now I

remember. I wonder about her story. We hear some wild ones in my line of work, Miss Vance."

"I'm sure you do, but I think Mrs. Keaton is telling the truth. In fact, I'd stake my reputation as an expert on battered women on it."

"Don't know if you should do that."

Michelle wasn't going to argue. She supposed people involved in law enforcement had reason to be skeptical of almost everyone they dealt with. Instead, she returned to the topic of the cut phone lines and the vandalism. "I guess you won't have much luck catching whoever did all this, will you?"

Officer Austin shrugged. "We might get lucky. I'll question the employees in the other offices and shops around here. Maybe someone saw something last night, but I wouldn't lay odds on it."

"Neither would I," Michelle murmured as they left the room. "But I'm sure you'll do your best."

"I sure will. And if you or your receptionist have any more trouble, just give us a call."

"Count on it." Michelle sank her top teeth into her lower lip and watched Officer Austin leave the office. She obviously assumed Doris Keaton was lying about why she'd shot her husband. Michelle could only hope a jury wouldn't think the same way.

At the end of the day Debbie approached Michelle's desk. "We're going to paint over the dirty words on the walls in the back room, but I could clean up the mess on the floor tonight. Want me to stay and do it?"

"No, go on home. We have a free hour in the morning. I can help you clear it out then. I can't tonight."

Debbie cocked her head to one side. "Why not? Hot date with your new main man?"

"What new main man?"

"Don't play dumb with me."

"I'm seeing Jon Wyatt this evening to discuss the threat you received and the vandalism."

"Uh-huh, and donkeys can fly."

"Just go home now," Michelle insisted, trying to look exasperated.

Chuckling knowingly, Debbie left.

After getting lost once in Raleigh, Michelle arrived at Jon's apartment at ten past seven. When he opened the double doors of the top floor apartment, she smiled apologetically. "Sorry I'm late. I turned down the wrong block a couple of stoplights back. Then I had to get back on course." She stepped into the foyer. "The penthouse, no less! I am impressed."

"I don't think you can really consider this a penthouse," he said wryly. "The building's not fancy enough to have one. I just happen to live at the top."

"It's very nice here, though," she told him as he led her into the living room, which was decorated in blue, ivory, and apricot. She nodded her approval. "This is a lovely room."

"Thanks. Let me take your raincoat." He helped her off with it, then hung it in a small closet to the right of the room. "You're not wet. They're predicting a big rain, but I guess it hasn't started yet."

"It was just beginning to drizzle when I got here."

"I think we have more to talk about than the weather," he said, smiling. "Put your purse down. I'll get us drinks and show you the rest of the place. Then I'll get back to making dinner. What would you like to drink? Sherry?"

"Perfect."

Still standing, she watched him walk over to the built-in bar, where he quickly poured two sherries. When he returned to hand her one glass, she looked him over with some amusement. "You look very handsome in your striped chef's apron."

He laughed. "My mother bought me this because she thinks I'm the world's untidiest cook."

"And are you?"

"Probably. At least a close second." Taking her free hand, he led her down the hall. "I don't usually give tours, but I want you to know exactly what this whole place looks like. Then when we're not together, you can imagine me wandering around through the rooms, pining for you."

"You're crazy," she said, laughing lightly. "I doubt I could ever imagine you pining for anyone or anything."

"You I could pine for," he insisted, looking down at her with a secret smile.

It was a large apartment for just one person, but it was comfortably and handsomely furnished. Michelle enjoyed seeing his study, with its profusion of law books; they lined most of two entire walls. Others were stacked haphazardly atop his massive oak desk.

"You must spend a lot of time in here," she commented. "Looks lived in."

"It's my favorite room."

Leading on, he showed her two small bedrooms,

107

then the master suite with its attached bath and dressing room. The moment he opened the door, he smiled rather sheepishly at her, then hurried to gather up a shirt and some socks from the floor. Wadding them all together, he took them to the hamper in the bathroom. Then he came back and said, "Sorry about that, but I got out of here in such a hurry this morning, I didn't have a chance to tidy up."

"Oh? You must wear a lot of socks at one time," she said with a grin, waving one hand toward his bed. "I see another pair under there. To be honest, Jon, I think you could use a housekeeper."

"I had one, but she said I made her job too hard. She left me to go work for a family with six children."

"I don't believe that."

"All right, she just wanted to retire," he admitted with a teasing smile. "She quit about two months ago, and I haven't had time to replace her yet."

After leaving the master bedroom, they went into the kitchen where Michelle gave an appreciative sniff. "Something sure smells delicious."

"My special secret spaghetti sauce," he said, releasing her hand to go over to the stove. "I hope you like spaghetti."

"Very much. Is there anything I can do to help?"

"You could do the salad. Everything you need is in the refrigerator."

As he stirred the sauce, she put her glass of sherry down on the wooden chopping block in the middle of the floor, then opened the refrigerator. From the crisper drawer, she took lettuce, a tomato, a cucumber, and a carrot. "I see you have a basket of mush-rooms in here. Want some in your salad?"

"Sure. Slice in a few."

"I'll add some to your plate later. I hate mush-rooms."

"Uh oh," he muttered, looking around at her. "We may want to go out to eat then. I put mushrooms in the spaghetti sauce."

Turning toward him, she shook her head. "No prob-lem. I'll just pick them out."

"You're sure?"

"Of course. If I eat one or two by mistake, it won't kill me. I don't actually hate mushrooms. I just don't care for the texture."

"I'll remember that and leave them out next time."

Next time. Michelle liked the sound of that.

As he cut thick slices of French bread to be lightly toasted, she washed lettuce leaves and tore them into bite-size pieces. She found a large wooden bowl in the first cabinet she opened and put the lettuce in it. As she sliced then diced the crisp tender cucumber, she hummed softly to herself.

"You sound happy for a woman who's just had her office vandalized," Jon said, coming over to stand be-side her at the chopping block. "And now that I've brought it up, let's talk about it now instead of spoiling dinner. Exactly what did the vandals do besides cut the phone lines?"

"Oh, there was trash thrown all over the floor, quite a lot of it. And they painted words on the walls."

"What words?"

"Obscene ones."

"Such as?"

"I'd really rather not say. I mean, I swear sometimes myself, but there were a couple words on the walls that I could never bring myself to utter. I've never even heard anyone say them. I've only read them in books."

"That bad, huh?" Jon's expression grew angry, and he slapped the chopping board with his left hand. "Damn. Sometimes I wish I hadn't gotten you involved in this case."

"Oh, don't be, really. I want to help Doris if I can. And I'm a big girl—I can handle this mess." Reaching over, she touched his hand. "You don't have to worry about me, Jon."

"Don't I?"

"No."

"Simply saying something doesn't make it so. I am worried about you. And Debbie. But especially you, because you're the one who's going to testify on Doris's behalf."

"And you're her lawyer, so if I'm in danger, so are you."

"But nobody's vandalized my office," he argued, then considered. "Of course, that would be difficult. I'm located in a building with an excellent security system. Guards patrol it day and night. But your office is never guarded, and there are only random police patrols on your street, I'm sure. And what about the police? I assume you talked to them. What did they say?"

"About what I expected. The policewoman who came to the office said she was going to see if anyone

110

might have noticed suspicious activity, but she didn't hold out much hope," Michelle said, then sighed heavily. "She—Officer Austin—bothered me, Jon. When she heard it was the Doris Keaton case I'd been warned to drop, she made it clear that she didn't believe Doris shot Vincent in self-defense. I know her work's probably made her jaded, but what if we can't convince a jury that Doris was protecting her life, either? That poor, sad woman will end up in prison, when it's really her husband who should be locked away."

"We're both going to try our best to see that it doesn't happen that way," Jon said quietly, slipping his fingers between hers and reassuringly squeezing them. "That's all we can do, Micki, our best. Now I'd better stir that sauce again before it sticks to the bottom of the pan."

Dinner was a success. As Jon poured two glasses of red wine, Michelle took her first bite of his spaghetti. "Um, delicious," she murmured, laughing when the end of one tender noodle escaped her fork and flicked a spot of tomato sauce on her upper lip. She patted it away with her napkin and added, "You said this is a secret recipe. Would you give it to me?"

His eyes narrowed. "Um, maybe. But you'd have to give something in return."

"What?"

"Can't you guess, my little chickadee?" he drawled, his tone theatrically wicked. "After all, I'm a normal hot-blooded American male."

"And a very presumptuous one," she said, trying to sound cool but having to smile a little nonetheless.

"Do you really think I'd surrender my honor for a spaghetti recipe?"

"Oh, I hope so."

She laughed, and he joined in.

After the meal, Michelle helped Jon load the dishwasher and tidy the kitchen. He had made quite a mess with his cooking. There were spatters of tomato sauce all over the top of the stove. "Your mother's right. You're very untidy in the kitchen," Michelle said, smiling.

"Great chefs don't worry about neatness."

"Most great chefs don't have to. They have assistants to clean up after them. You don't."

"Go ahead then, criticize. Forget you've just had the best spaghetti you've ever eaten in your life," Jon complained, employing wildly dramatic gestures. "And you'll never taste any that's better."

"You've got to do something to build up your self-confidence," Michelle teased as she used a small soapy cloth to wash out the sink.

Their chores were finished a few minutes later, and they returned to the cozy living room. Michelle hung back in the doorway as Jon proceeded across the floor. Suddenly she wondered why she had ever decided to come here, knowing he would likely be doubly dangerous on his own turf. He was a very persuasive man anyplace, anytime, but here and now . . . Her heart began to hammer. Maybe she liked him too much. Maybe she was even beginning to fall in love. Maybe she should just get the hell home right away and avoid a situation that could ultimately cause her great pain.

Swallowing hard, she took a deep breath and took

two steps forward, glancing at her watch. It was only a few minutes past nine, but she said, her words tumbling nervously out, "I know it's rude to eat and run, but it's getting late and I have some work at home I need to do."

"Work, work, work," he gently chastised, coming back to take both her hands in his as his magnetic eyes held hers. "How long is it going to take me to teach you that you have to play sometimes, too, if you want to be a whole, well-rounded person?"

"Look, Jon, I—"

"Quiet. Come here." He led her to the sliding glass doors that opened onto his terrace and overlooked the beautifully lighted city. Hard rain fell in sheets against the terrace tiles. His gaze was warm and concerned as he looked down at her. "I can't let you drive home in that. It's pouring, and you could have an accident. You should stay here until it slackens off some. We'll relax and talk and listen to some soft music."

As if mesmerized by his deep musical voice, she agreed that it was dangerous to try to drive in a deluge. She allowed him to lead her to the blue sofa in the middle of the room. He left her to go put a record on the stereo, then returned to sit down close beside her as a love ballad instrumental began.

"Want to dance?" he asked a few moments later. When she nodded, he stood, took her hands, and drew her to her feet.

It felt good to be in his arms again, and she rested her head against his shoulder. She closed her eyes and relaxed as they moved slowly in time with the music.

"You're a very graceful dancer," he said, his lips moving over her hair.

"That tickles," she murmured.

"Does it?" he murmured back. "How about this?" Tilting her head to the right, he scattered nuzzling little kisses along the left side of her neck. "This tickle, too?"

"No, that makes me tingle."

"Good, we're making progress."

Opening her eyes, she leaned her head back to look at him. "I thought we were supposed to be dancing, not making progress."

"We can do both at the same time. Now, kiss me."

"Jon—"

"Micki, kiss me," he coaxed softly. "Now."

Suddenly she realized she had been wanting to do just that all evening. Stretching up on tiptoe, she pressed her lips against his. When he groaned and pulled her closer, her arms tightened around him. She felt almost faint as his mouth took potent possession of hers. Boldly, she played the tip of her tongue over his.

Passion exploded in him, and he could nearly feel it radiating from her. "Micki, honey," he whispered, then swept her up in his arms and carried her out of the room.

She knew where he was taking her but couldn't stop him, didn't want to. At the moment it felt right to allow her desires to intensify. It was only when he lowered her to his bed and leaned over her that she began to wonder if she was ready yet for complete intimacy with him. "Maybe I was crazy to let you

114

bring me in here," she said, looking deeply into his eyes. "M-maybe I should go home now."

"Don't go," he whispered. "Spend the night with me, Micki."

It was difficult to breathe properly, although his request hadn't surprised her. She had known when she'd come here tonight that he would probably ask her to stay. She had known but had come anyway. What she didn't know now was whether to say no or yes.

CHAPTER SEVEN

"I don't know if I should stay, Jon," Michelle said at last. "I really don't know."

"You want to spend the night with me, don't you?"

"Well, yes, in a way, but—"

"I really can't allow you to drive home. You've been drinking."

"I've had two drinks," she said wryly. "You know very well I'm sober. And maybe I should get home to the cat."

"You told me yourself she has a way to get in and out of the house, and I'm sure you left food in her dish. Stop looking for excuses to leave and say you'll stay."

Her wry smile faded. "Jon, sex can't be a casual thing for me."

"Believe me, Micki, my feelings for you are far more than casual," he said sincerely. "But I guess I'm just going to have to convince you."

His long lean body pressed her down into the softness of the mattress. His warm lips claimed hers and commenced an arousing onslaught on her senses. When he turned over onto his side, taking her with him, and began exploring her body with his questing hands, she moaned and pressed closer to him.

"Say yes," he murmured, kissing her neck.

"Oh, Jon!"

"Say yes," he repeated, nibbling the tender lobe of her ear. "Say yes, Micki."

"Yes," she breathed, unable to resist him any longer. When he pulled back slightly, she opened her eyes and saw a glint of triumph flash in the green depths of his. She smiled softly. "I do want to spend the night with you."

"We'll be good together."

"I know."

He stroked her brow with the edge of one thumb. "Now, here's what I want you to do. Go into my bathroom and put on the gorilla suit you'll find in there. Then come back out here and chase me around the room a few times. That really turns me on."

Stunned, she stared at him. "What?"

"Just kidding," he said, and had to laugh. "You should have seen how big your eyes got."

"You devil!" she cried, and retaliated for the joke by tickling him. And at that moment she knew she was in love with him.

A few moments later, after he had captured both her hands to keep them away from his ribs, he asked, "Wouldn't you be willing to play games with me?"

"Depends on what kind of games. I draw the line at dressing in a gorilla suit."

"I don't even own one."

"I'm relieved to hear that. What made you say such an outrageous thing to me, anyway?"

"I hoped a little humor would help you relax," he said, running his fingers through her hair. "You seemed a little tense and uncertain. You don't now."

"I'm not," she whispered, cupping his beloved face in her hands and moving nearer to kiss him.

Their kisses lengthened and deepened and were soon not nearly enough for either of them. Slowly, sensuously, in the soft circle of lamplight, they undressed each other, touching and caressing all the while. When they were both naked, Jon lay facing her, devouring her lovely body with his darkening gaze. "God, Micki, you're beautiful."

Eyes dreamy, lips parted, she felt on fire all over. He didn't even have to touch her to make her melt. All he had to do was look at her the way he was. The love she felt for him became an ache that had nothing to do with sexual need, although she was definitely experiencing that, too. But the emotion of love, all by itself, was almost painful as it seemed to gather in the center of her chest. Her breath quickened. "Jon, oh Jon," she whispered throatily, curving one hand over the back of his neck, urging him to kiss her again. "Love me. Love me. Now."

"Oh yes, I'm going to," he whispered back as his arms went tenderly around her.

His roaming hands made her wild, and his lips kissing her all over made her burn. Through half-closed eyes, she watched his lean fingers move between her thighs to caress her intimately. The central physical ache in her was now an emptiness that only he could fill. She gasped softly with keen pleasure as his mouth toyed with her breasts and his lips, teeth, and tongue teased her sensitized nipples.

Although she was femininely acquiescent, she played an active role in their lovemaking, adding immensely to Jon's excitement. Her slender hands were as exploring and caressing as his, and a tremor ran over him when she lightly raked her nails down his back over his naked hips.

White-hot passion flowed between them, very close to becoming out of control. With all the self-discipline he could muster, he pulled away from her. "If we don't think about taking precautions now, Micki, we won't be able to soon." He smiled sensuously. "I'll go get what we need."

Shaking her head, she feathered her fingertips over his firm jaw. "You don't have to. I'm on the Pill."

He raised his eyebrows. "Oh, really?"

Her smile became indulgent. "Now, don't go thinking I sleep around, because I don't. My doctor prescribed the Pill for a minor problem I have."

"How minor?"

"Very. Mostly a monthly aggravation."

"Thank God for that."

The sincerity conveyed by those four words made her love for him increase tenfold. He did care about her—perhaps very much.

"Well, now that I know we're safe, where were we?" he asked teasingly. "Ah yes, I was kissing your eyelids, and you were about to do this." He drew her hands down between them, sighing with delight as her fingers curved around him, stroking.

Only a few minutes later, he uttered roughly, "I have to have you, Micki. I can't wait."

"Oh yes, darling," she murmured, a shiver of sweet pleasure arrowing through her. "Come to me now, Jon."

"Oh, my sweet," he said, raising her parted knees and moving between them. As he lowered himself down, his eyes held hers. He gave her a gentle smile as she involuntarily took a sharp breath. "Relax, honey. I'm going to be very gentle."

She nodded, knowing he would be. It was mainly the seriousness of the commitment she was about to make that had made her breath catch. And she whispered, "Yes, oh yes," when his hardness brushed throbbingly against her.

They were still looking into each other's eyes when, with a tender thrust, he entered the sleek sheath of her inner warmth. Then they kissed as she arched up against him, and he stroked deeper and higher, deeper and higher, until he filled her completely. Then he was still, delighting in the feminine flesh enclosing him. She pressed her fingertips hard against the taut muscles of his shoulders. He whispered in her ear, "Good?"

"Hm, so good, Jon."

"Yes, so very good, honey." He began to move slowly up and down within her.

They made love slowly, thoroughly enjoying each other. Michelle began to dreamily feel as if no one else existed in the world except the two of them. It was a magical feeling.

"Think I could convince you to wear a gorilla suit

for me now?" Jon asked after a while. "I mean, while I have you under my power?"

"No, I don't think you could," she answered, her laughter light and lilting. "Not even now."

Soon the fluttering sensations he was creating in her came faster and faster with more intensity. Her breathing troubled, she clung to him, needing ultimate fulfillment.

Sensing her need, driven by his own, Jon lost control and began taking her with sure yet gentle swiftness.

With a soft cry she was swept upward to the piercing pinnacle of physical ecstasy. As Jon joined her there, she wrapped her arms and legs tightly around them as they both tumbled over the edge and floated down into warm completion.

A few minutes later, as they lay holding each other and their heartbeats slowed to normal again, he smoothed her tousled hair back from her face. "Now, that wasn't so bad, was it?"

"Not so bad," she teased, nuzzling her lips against his right shoulder. "You did okay."

"What do you mean, okay?"

"Well, better than okay."

"Keep going."

"All right, you were terrific."

"And just think about how you've been fighting this since the first day we met."

"It was worth the wait, don't you think?"

"I sure do, Micki," he said, kissing her temples. "But it would've been just as good if you'd let it happen the last time we were together."

"No, because I wasn't ready then. Tonight I was."

"You certainly were." Smiling at her, he started to move off the bed. "We were in such a hurry, we didn't even get under the covers. Guess we'd better do that now."

She hesitated a moment. "Maybe I should go home."

"Why? It's nearly midnight. Why drive so far this late?"

She grinned. "Because if I go into work tomorrow wearing the same thing I wore today, Debbie's sure to notice, and she'll know I spent the night with you. Believe me, I'll never hear the end of it."

"Problem solved. I'll set the clock so we can get up early enough for you to go home and change your clothes. Debbie will never know." Taking her hands, he pulled her off the bed and into his arms. "Come on, admit it. You'd rather stay here with me where it's warm than drive home in that cold rain. Right?"

"You talked me into it," she said, happier then than she had ever been, gesturing toward the bed.

They pulled up the covers together. Jon reached over to switch off the lamp on the bedside table. They snuggled up, and soon afterward, as the rain beat against the windows, they drifted off to sleep.

The next morning, Jon tried to wake Michelle at about six thirty but had very little success.

"What are you doing?" she mumbled sleepily. "It's got to be too early."

"It's six thirty."

She moaned. "Cripes, it's not even light outside, and you're trying to drag me out of bed!"

"You wanted to get up in time to go home and change clothes before you got to your office. Rise and shine, Micki."

"No way," she muttered, turning over and hiding her head under her pillow.

Remembering she had told him she was always grumpy in the morning, Jon smiled wryly and went into the kitchen to make coffee. A few minutes later, he returned to the bedroom with two hot mugfuls. Sipping from one, he sat down on the edge of the bed. Gently he poked her back with his left elbow. "I'm not giving up, Micki. Get your head out from under that pillow. I've brought you coffee."

Moaning again, she slowly and reluctantly pulled the pillow aside and blinked her eyes as she looked up at him. "You're a cruel man, Jonathan Wyatt. When I said I wanted to leave early, I didn't mean you had to wake me up in the middle of the night."

"Don't exaggerate." He held out the mug in his left hand. "Here, have this. Pick you right up."

Grumbling, she sat up. Before she remembered she was naked, the covers slipped down to her waist, baring her breasts. Faintly blushing, she hurriedly pulled them back up around her.

"You don't have to cover up," Jon said wryly. "I won't mind if you don't."

"I'm sure. But I'd feel at a disadvantage. After all, you're in a robe." Taking the mug, she hurriedly took one sip of coffee, then another, hoping to soon feel human again. She eyed him over the rim. "How long have you been up?"

"About twenty minutes. Long enough to shave."

"But why the hell did you want to get up this early?"

"You really are cranky in the morning, aren't you?"

"Yes. And you didn't answer my question."

His half-smile broadened. "All right, I wanted us to have time to take a shower together before you leave for Chapel Hill."

"You're kidding!" she exclaimed, shaking her head. "Don't you know what that would lead to?"

"Of course I know. That's why it's such a fine idea."

"Uh-unh, no way."

"Just be quiet and drink your coffee. Once you have some caffeine in you, you'll change your mind."

Her eyes narrowed as she looked at him. "You're very sure of yourself."

"I just know you enjoyed last night as much as I did."

As the memory of their lovemaking swept through her, she mellowed slightly but tried not to show it. "I did enjoy what we had together, but that doesn't mean I'm going to shower with you this morning."

"We'll see," he drawled, and winked. "I'm a persuasive man."

"You're out of luck this time, though," she declared. When he chuckled in response, she glared at him.

After a second mug of coffee, Michelle reverted from grump to pleasant person again. The idea of showering with Jon did hold more appeal now, but she still intended not to let him persuade her to do it. She wasn't sure why; maybe things were simply moving at too fast a pace. It was only last night when she had truly realized she was in love with him. They had made love once, and she was a little afraid that if they did it again so soon, she might become so deeply committed that she could end up getting hurt. Then again, maybe it was too late to worry about that.

She smiled unsurely at Jon, wondering exactly what he did feel for her.

"Aha, I can tell by your expression that the coffee has vanquished the morning monster," he said, a hint of laughter in his voice. "I knew I only had to be patient."

She glanced around the room. "Would you happen to have a robe I could wear?"

"Yes, and I'll take it into the bathroom for you to put on after our shower."

"Jon, I need it now. I'd like to go to the bathroom. And please tell me you have a spare toothbrush I can use."

"I always keep a couple of new ones in the medicine cabinet," he said, going to his walk-in closet. He took down a terry-cloth robe, which he tossed to her. "Just grab one."

The robe, naturally sized to fit him, swallowed Michelle up. She wound it around her, tied the belt at her waist, and then had to hold the hem up to keep from tripping over it as she walked into the bathroom and shut the door. A minute or so later, she stood before the mirror and gazed at her reflection. Despite her tousled hair, she looked good. Her eyes were bright, and there was a tint of healthy color in her cheeks.

"You look happy," she said to her mirror image, and knew in that instant that she felt happy indeed.

Jon was sitting up against the headboard of the bed when she came back out of the bathroom. She gave him a quick smile, then looked around. "If I can find my clothes, I'll get dressed and out of here."

"You won't find them," he announced with an unabashed grin. "I hid them."

"Hid them! You didn't!"

"I did."

"Stop this foolishness and give them back!"

"I have my heart set on taking a shower with you, so just accept the inevitable, Micki. If you don't, I'll toss you over my shoulder and carry you into that bathroom."

"You wouldn't!"

"Watch me." Slowly, smiling lazily, he moved off the bed and toward her.

Raw excitement rushed through her. He meant it! Holding up one hand as if to ward him off, she took backward steps. "Stop where you are. Don't touch me. If you do, I'll bite and kick," she warned, knowing full well that the threat she issued was an empty one.

Jon knew it, too. "No, you won't. You want to take a shower with me, but for some reason you're fighting your own desire. I'm not going to let you do that." Moving quickly, he strode across the room, picked her up, and took her into the bathroom.

Michelle had to laugh, even as she pretended to resist. It had become a game now—one she found she very much liked. Jon put her down to open the glass doors of the tub, and when he bent over slightly to

126

turn on the faucets and adjust the temperature of the water, his arm around her waist loosened a bit.

"See you," she sang out victoriously, slipping free of his hold and running back into the bedroom.

Jon gave chase, grinning when he saw she was searching for her clothes—or at least pretending to. "You won't find them in here. I hid them in another room."

Close to giggling, she tried to make a dash for the door to the hall. When he blocked the way and tried to reach out and grab hold of her robe, she dodged him and sped around behind the easy chair by the window. He followed. She faked left, then ran to the right. For a full five minutes she adroitly evaded capture as excitement mounted. Then she was laughing too hard and was finally cornered beside the chest of drawers.

"Gotcha," Jon said, laughing, too, and stepping forward to enfold her in his arms. "Now you're mine again, woman."

And she felt as if she belonged to him. She brushed her lips over his. Their laughter ceased. Whispering her name, he slipped his hands beneath the lapels of the terry robe and fondled her firm round breasts. He murmured, "Let's go take that shower now."

Under the foamy spray of the shower head, they caressed each other with soapy hands that played intimately and gently, arousing them both to wondrous heights of desire. Michelle's legs went weak after he rinsed her off and his mouth enclosed the peaks of her wet breasts.

"Oh, Jon," she breathed. "Take me back to bed."

"Yes. Now," he muttered, turning off the water and

helping her out of the tub to rub her down with a thick towel. She did the same for him. Then they slipped their arms around each other's waists and walked out of the bathroom.

Nearly an hour later, Michelle convinced Jon to return her hidden clothes. After he did, she dressed quickly, knowing that only if she hurried would she have time to go home and change and still get to her office on time.

Jon walked her to the door, gently clasped her shoulders, and lowered his head to kiss her. "Will I see you tonight?"

"I hope so," she murmured, adoring him. "What time?"

"About seven?"

"Fine. I'll make dinner."

"No, let's go out."

"What? You don't like my cooking?"

"It's not that at all. I just think you need to relax more."

"Well, I'm certainly not going to refuse a free meal," she said wryly. "I'll be ready at seven, then."

They kissed once again then he let her go.

He didn't arrive at her house at seven o'clock, but by then Michelle was no longer expecting him. About five thirty, his secretary had called her at the office and told her he was involved in an urgent matter and wouldn't be able to see her that night. Michelle, though disappointed, understood.

Her understanding slipped to nil, though, when another four days passed and she didn't hear a word from Jon or even get a message from him through his secretary. She felt betrayed, hurt, angry. It was obvious that he had gotten what he'd wanted from her—sex—and was now no longer interested.

"Nitwit," she called herself on the fourth day, determined not to cry. After all, she had brought all this on herself. She had known as soon as she met him that he might be trouble, yet still she had let herself fall in love.

CHAPTER EIGHT

On Sunday, Michelle and Debbie went to the office to paint the walls of the back room. Although the office was the property of the state of North Carolina, they had agreed that the job would get done faster if they did it themselves.

"Thanks for helping pay for the paint," Michelle said while prying the lid off a can. "You didn't have to."

"Heck, I would've been willing to pay the whole cost," Debbie answered, taking two rollers and a paint pan out of a paper bag. "You know how many miles of red tape I would've had to go through to get someone from the state to do this? And it might have been a year or more before anyone came. I'm very tired of seeing the dirty words some deviant scrawled on the walls."

"Sorry we have to do it on Sunday, though. I hope you didn't have plans for this afternoon."

"Not really. Bobby is playing touch football with some of his friends, and frankly, I'm always bored to death when I have to watch their games."

"Why don't you play with them? That would be more fun."

"Ha, not for me it wouldn't. I'm not the athletic type. For me, getting physical means lifting my hands far enough above my head to roll my hair."

Michelle smiled disbelievingly. "You can't be that inactive."

"Wanna bet?"

The screwdriver Michelle was using to pry the can lid off suddenly slipped, and the sharp tip jabbed painfully into her thumb. "Damnation!" she cried, dropping the tool with a clatter and putting her thumb into her mouth.

Debbie hurried over. "Is it bad? Did you break the skin?"

Taking her thumb out of her mouth, Michelle shook her head. "It isn't bleeding—just throbbing a little now. It's a big deal only because I don't want anymore trouble right now, no matter how minor."

"What's wrong, Michelle?" Debbie asked soberly. "You haven't been yourself for a few days. Something's going on. What's the matter? Does it have anything to do with Jon Wyatt?"

Michelle glanced up at her receptionist, then quickly looked back down. "What makes you ask that?"

"It's just that he hasn't been around or even called you for a while."

"So you've noticed that, too, have you?" Michelle murmured rather bitterly.

"Did you two have an argument or something?"

"Not that I know of." Remembering exactly how

she and Jon had spent their last hour together—in bed —Michelle closed her eyes briefly and shook her head. "No, nothing as dramatic as an argument. I guess he just lost interest in me."

"I can hardly believe that. I mean, I saw how he acted toward you, and—"

"And people's actions can sometimes be very deceiving."

Debbie sighed. "I can tell you're really upset."

"I'll live."

"He was really beginning to get to you, wasn't he? You really like him?"

"You could say that," Michelle muttered, not adding that that would be an understatement.

Debbie perked up. "Oh, he'll call you again soon, I know he will."

"Of course he will. He'll have to, because I'm going to testify for Doris Keaton."

"No, I mean he'll call you for personal reasons."

"You're such an optimist, Deb."

"Well, I have to admit, men can be pains sometimes. I mean, Bobby can be so dreadfully inconsiderate once in a while," the younger woman confided, then shrugged. "Of course, I have my faults, too."

"We all do," said Michelle, wondering if perhaps she had been too reserved with Jon, not affectionate enough to satisfy him. But that was a laugh. How much more affection could a reserved person show than making love passionately and practically without inhibition? She shrugged. "Ah well, as I said, I'll live."

"Right. If things don't work out with Jon, there are a lot of other fish in the sea."

"Yes, indeed. Now let's stop this dilly-dallying. I'll stir the paint while you put down the drop cloths. Then we'll get to work."

"Aye aye, skipper," Debbie said, smiling comfortingly as she gave a brisk salute.

On Monday morning, Michelle received a very pleasant surprise. Doris Keaton came to the office—quite a feat for a woman who had previously been afraid to leave her sister's house. When Debbie showed her into the private office, Michelle greeted her with a big smile. "Oh, I'm so glad to see you here, Doris! You are making progress—I knew you would. Please sit down."

Taking the visitor's chair by Michelle's desk, Doris smiled back tremulously and smoothed the skirt of her dress. "I know I don't have an appointment, but I was afraid that if I made one, I'd chicken out and not come. I decided I'd just better do it, so here I am. I hope I'm not inconveniencing you."

"Not at all. I'm free for the next twenty minutes. I can't tell you how glad I am you built up enough self-confidence to come."

"Well, I didn't exactly come alone. I mean, I couldn't face the thought of doing that yet. I asked Anna to drive me, and she did. She's going to shop while I'm with you, then pick me up here in about a half an hour."

Michelle nodded. "Just coming here was an important step for you to make, Doris. You must be feeling better."

"A little more every day. I decided that since

Vincent's still in the hospital, he can't hurt me, and it was silly of me to keep hiding in Anna's house. After all, I'm on my own now, and I have to start trying to be stronger. That's why I could never force myself to leave him—I was terrified of being out on my own."

"I know. That's not unusual in your situation."

Doris heaved a sigh. "I've been thinking about joining your therapy group. I think maybe it would help me, but I'm still not quite ready yet."

"When you're ready, give me a call, and I'll tell you when the next meeting is," Michelle said patiently. "And I want you to know that most of the women I see are reluctant to join at first. You're not an exception."

They talked productively until it was time for Michelle's next appointment. Then Doris went out to wait for her sister in the reception area. Preparing for her next client, Michelle smiled to herself, heartened by the progress Doris was making. She felt that the woman soon would feel strong enough to face trial, but naturally that was a decision her psychiatrist would ultimately make.

Unfortunately, Michelle's day ran downhill after her meeting with Doris. All the clients she saw were seriously considering reuniting with the men who had abused them. All except one, who was close to having a nervous breakdown because she was having such difficulty providing for herself and her three children.

Relieved when the long day ended, Michelle said good night to Debbie at the door, locked the office, and drove home. There things got even worse. She let herself in, and then stood stock still in the living room when she saw that her very own home had been vandalized.

"Oh, God! Oh, my God!" she uttered raspingly, reading the horrible obscenities that had been painted in stark black on the cream-colored walls. A painting, a signed reproduction, that she had loved and saved for months to buy had been slashed to ribbons. All at once, it was too much: Jon's betrayal; her bad day; and now this! Tears cascaded down her cheeks. Then they stopped briefly when she remembered Winston Churchill. Had the cat been in the house when the vandal broke in? The animal wasn't fond of strangers, had once even tried to attack a door-to-door salesman who had seemed a bit threatening. What if she had attacked whoever did this?

"If you hurt my cat, I'll find you somehow, and—" And what? Michelle didn't really know what she'd do. She ran over the house, searching for her cat.

She breathed a big sigh of relief when she finally found Winnie curled up, peacefully asleep, on the end of her bed. Obviously the cat had been outside when the vandalism occurred or had simply slept through it. Sinking down onto the edge of the bed, Michelle petted Winnie, who woke up with a start and spat at her.

"Okay, so you're hungry. That's no reason to be vicious," Michelle scolded, moving her hand away and feeling tempted to spit back. But she didn't. Instead, she went to call the police.

An officer came quickly—a man this time. He surveyed the damage, and once again she explained the case she was working on and the warnings she had received to drop it. Once again she was told there was little possibility that the vandal would be tracked down. After thanking the policeman and showing him out, she closed and locked the front door, leaned back against it, and rubbed her tired eyes. Days like this one she could certainly do without.

Sipping a brandy, she made soup and salad for dinner. But she was only about halfway through her meal when her phone rang. With a weary sigh she went to answer it, hoping it wouldn't be her mother, who faithfully called her once a week. If it was her, Michelle wasn't sure she could pretend to be upbeat. Her mother knew her too well to be fooled by an act, but she didn't want her parents to worry about her.

It wasn't Michelle's mother on the phone. It was Jon. "I just got in and found my apartment vandalized," he told her hurriedly. "My first thought was of you. Anything happen at your house?"

"As a matter of fact, I have obscenities all over my living-room walls," she said coldly, trying to ignore the ache that materialized in the center of her chest at the sound of his voice. "Quite a welcome home, I must say."

"Then you just got there?" he asked.

"No. I've been home since about five thirty."

"What?" he questioned, confused. "But I checked with my secretary, and she didn't mention any messages from you. Didn't you try to call me to tell me what happened?"

"Why should I do that?" she asked brusquely.

"What's that mean?"

"I think you know exactly what it means," she said,

136

managing to keep her voice steady. Then she hung up on him.

"Damn," Jon said, striking his forehead with the heel of his hand. "She's mad because I haven't been in touch. I can't really blame her, but after I explain, she'll understand."

Worried about her house being vandalized, too, he walked into his bedroom. The thought of her being alone there bothered him immensely, but he knew he'd never be able to persuade the police in Chapel Hill to provide round-the-clock protection for her. There was only one thing to do. Luckily he hadn't unpacked this evening when he'd returned from New York, and there were still fresh clothes in his suitcase. He walked to the foot of his bed, picked up his suitcase, and started out.

Still stewing over his call, Michelle sat on her sofa, her legs crossed, one foot bobbing up and down. "Some nerve," she muttered to herself.. "Calling up as if nothing had happened, as if he'd just talked to me this afternoon." She wished she had told him exactly what she thought of him instead of getting so angry and upset that she'd hung up. When she had another chance, she was going to burn his ears off. He deserved to hear a few choice words.

"Forget him," she told herself. "Treat yourself to a bubble bath."

But the bath didn't help much. The warm water and frothy bubbles relaxed her physically, but forgetting Jon wasn't as easy. She knew her anger was defensive, brought about by the hurt he had caused. Tears filled her eyes again, but she willed them away. She had already cried once tonight, and once was enough.

After a half-hour soak, feeling slightly better, she got out of the tub, toweled dry, and slipped into her white gown, her comfortably worn blue fleece robe, and her fuzzy slippers.

Winne stood on a chair and meowed beseechingly as Michelle walked back into the living room to read. Michelle shook her head. "No way am I going to scratch your rump. You're in the doghouse, too. I'm tired of you spitting at me."

The cat stared placidly back at her.

"And don't look so blasé," her mistress added. "At least a dog would know to look ashamed."

Winnie kept staring as if to say, "What do you expect? I am a cat, not a dog, and cats never let humans bother them."

Her expression disgusted, Michelle started toward the bookcase. Then the doorbell rang, startling her. Ever since she had come home and found the place vandalized, she had jumped at every unexpected sound. Pressing her hand against her chest, she took two big breaths to slow her racing heartbeat. With mounting trepidation she approached the front door. Ever since she had become involved in the Doris Keaton case, she never knew what might happen. Who could be standing outside on the porch right now? Could it be the man who had been threatening and harassing her? She wasn't about to just pull the door open.

"Wh-who is it?" she called out.

"It's Jon."

She tensed. For an instant she was tempted to tell him to get lost, but she remembered she had an earful to give him. Undoing the double-bolt lock, then unfastening the chain, she swung the door open, glared briefly at Jon, and turned around and marched away.

Grimacing, he stepped across the threshold, shut the door, and relocked it; then he followed her. When he put his hands on her squared shoulders, she shrugged them off. He sighed.

"I know you're miffed at me, and you have a right to be," he said quietly. "But I can explain. I was called to New York unexpectedly, and all the time I was there I was constantly busy. I planned to call you several times, but something else always came up to prevent me from doing it. I'm sorry. Forgive me?"

"No," she said, her voice steely. "Your explanation's not good enough. You could have called me if you'd really wanted to."

"You don't understand how busy I was. I barely got four hours of sleep every night I was there. And when I got back to my hotel room, it was too late to call here. I didn't want to wake you up. Try to understand that."

She spun around to face him, rosy anger unfurling in flags on her cheeks. "I understand that you got what you wanted from me, then lost interest."

"That's not true," he murmured, reaching out his hand toward her again and dropping it when she took a step back. His steady gaze held hers. "Micki, I'm sorry you think that, because you're dead wrong. I certainly haven't lost interest in you."

"Haven't you? Then why do I feel so used?"

"You shouldn't. I'd never use you."

"I think you already have," she muttered. She wanted to believe him, but somehow she couldn't allow herself to. Too much was at stake to take a chance. She looked at him accusingly. "You chased me down, got me into your bed, then decided I wasn't that special after all."

"Don't say that! Don't even think it!" he said, his face anguished and contrite. "All right, I admit I was inconsiderate, but—"

"Inconsiderate is not the word for it. Debbie thinks her fiancé is inconsiderate sometimes, but he couldn't hold a candle to you."

Wearily, Jon loosened his tie and unbuttoned his collar. He asked, "Don't you believe in giving a fellow a second chance?"

She was relentless. "I've seen too many women give men second chances."

"For God's sake, Micki, I simply failed to call you and tell you I was in New York for a few days. Listen, I know now I hurt your feelings, but—"

"I'm not hurt," she lied coolly, unwilling to let him know he could hurt her, that she cared that much about him. "I'm just damned mad."

"I can see that," he answered, giving up for the time being. It was obvious she was in no mood to listen to reason at the moment. He would give her a chance to cool off and be more objective. He smiled tiredly. "We'll talk about this later."

"I don't see why we should."

"Well, I do, and we will talk," he said, his voice growing stern. "That's a promise."

A promise she chose to ignore. She asked instead, "What are you doing here, Jon?"

For the first time he looked around the room and saw the words scrawled on the walls. "My God, you got it worse than I did. *Bastard* and *s.o.b.* were about the worst thing on mine. How did the vandals get in here?"

"The police said through one of my bedroom windows."

Jon frowned. "You must be scared."

She shrugged. "I'll survive."

Since she was being impossible, he decided to delay telling her why he had come tonight. He glanced at the sofa. "Let's sit down. Would it be too much trouble for me to have a brandy?"

Her inbred southern hospitality won out over her desire to refuse him a drink. But when she handed him a glass, she sat down on the far end of the sofa, a none-too-gracious look on her face.

He saw her hands were empty. "Aren't you going to join me?"

"No, we aren't going to be having any more social encounters. We're going back to a strictly professional relationship."

"Micki, for God's sake, I—"

"You still haven't told me why you came here."

With an irritated curse beneath his breath, he put his brandy down, got up, opened the door, and picked up his suitcase. He brought it in, then closed and relocked the door again.

Michelle eyed the bag suspiciously. "What's that for?"

"Just a few of my things. I'm moving in with you until the Keaton trial is over."

"Oh no, you're not!" Leaping to her feet, Michelle planted her hands on her hips and shook her head. "You're crazy!"

He lost all patience. Being overworked in New York had nearly exhausted him. He didn't intend to get into yet another argument with Michelle. He dropped the suitcase to the floor without noticing that the cat's eyes flew open and stared wildly when it bumped loudly on the wood. His own eyes were on Michelle and narrowing as he strode over to grab her wrists in a tight grip. When she tried to pull free, he wouldn't let go.

"I know you're mad at me right now, but this is something we're not going to argue about," he said, his voice nearly a growl. "I'm not letting you stay by yourself until the trial's over and you're out of danger. I'm staying here with you."

She glared up at him. "I don't need you to look after me. I can take care of myself. I'll buy a gun if I have to."

"And have you ever handled one?"

"Well, no, but—"

"Then you'd probably shoot your foot off if you ever had to use one—especially if someone was breaking in here in the middle of the night and you panicked. But I've handled guns—there's one in that suitcase over there. The police can't protect you, and I can. So you have only two choices: Either I stay here with you, or you move in with me. Got that?"

She got it. Judging by the determined look in his

eyes, she could see he meant what he said and wouldn't change his mind, no matter how long and hard she might argue. Secretly, she had to admit she would feel safer with him in the house at night. Although their strained relationship would make her extremely uneasy with him, she would feel less threatened by the unknown man who was constantly intensifying his harassment.

But she wasn't going to admit that to Jon. "All right, stay then, even if I don't need your protection. But you're going to have to sleep on the sofa. I warn you, it's mighty uncomfortable. You're going to be sorry." Her eyes shifted to his hands on her wrists. "Now, will you let go? You're hurting me, and you know I won't put up with that."

His eyes darkened as he immediately loosened his grip. "I'm sorry."

"That's what they all say. Then they do something worse," she muttered sarcastically. "Next time you'll probably hit me."

"You're being ridiculous," he snapped, releasing her wrists completely, "and you know it."

"Don't tell me what I know or don't know."

"Good God, woman, you would try the patience of a saint," he said, shaking his head. "Now, I don't want to seem rude, but do you think I could have something to eat? I haven't had dinner."

After heating up the remainder of the soup, she made him a ham and cheese sandwich and left him in the kitchen to eat it. "I'll make up the sofa for you. Then I'm going to bed."

"Hope you're in a better mood in the morning," he said, shaking his head and taking a sip of milk.

Breakfast was tense. Michelle was very quiet; Jon could tell she was still put out with him. And it seemed that every muscle in his body ached. She had been right about that sofa; it was hellishly uncomfortable. He thought sleeping on a bed of nails would have been better.

For Michelle, breakfast with Jon was a torment. It should have been an intimate time, yet she felt very much alone, alienated from him. It hurt to know that if he cared more about her, it would have been different.

Jon was biding his time, feeling sure he could win her over again eventually. He had been inconsiderate; he should have called her from New York, even in the middle of the night if necessary. But he hadn't, and that was a mistake. But surely she wouldn't hold one mistake against him forever. He knew he would have to proceed cautiously. She was suspicious of all men because she worked with abused women and because she had once been involved with a man who had slapped her. Difficult as it was going to be, he had to be patient.

Nibbling on a strip of bacon, Michelle suppressed a sigh. Their conversation was sparse and stilted, mainly concerning world events. They said nothing personal. Halfway through her eggs and bacon, her appetite nonexistent, she got an excuse to stop eating when Winnie sauntered up from the basement, looking as ill-tempered as she usually did before she had a meal.

Steering clear of the cat, she filled the bowl on the floor, then glanced over at Jon and excused herself.

After she finished in the bathroom, he went in to shower, shave, and dress. She dressed in her bedroom. By coincidence, they walked out into the short hall at the same time. They went on into the living room. Both carried briefcases. Avoiding his eyes, Michelle opened the front door, stuck her nose out, and shivered. "Brrr, it's chilly out this morning," she said with a deliberately light tone. She took her all-weather coat off the wooden tree by the door. "Hope you brought a coat to wear today."

"No, but I'll be fine. I'll stop by my apartment on my way here from my office this evening and pick up a few things I need," he said, moving across the room to stand before her. "Micki, I want you and Debbie to stay together when you're at work. If both of you can't go out for lunch at the same time, order in. And I'm going to drive you to the office every day and pick you up."

"No, I can't let you do that. I need to have my car. Sometimes a client will call with an emergency, and I have to go to her."

A muscle ticked in his tight jaw. "I don't like it, but if you insist—"

"I do."

"All right. But I still want you and Debbie to arrive at the office at the same time and leave together, too. Understand?"

"I understand, master," she said defensively, loving him, wanting to reach out and touch him, yet knowing she couldn't. "Your will is my command."

"Sarcasm doesn't suit you," he responded tersely, wanting to take her in his arms and carry her to bed again. But he knew she'd fight him tooth and nail if he tried. "Just stay with Debbie during the day, and I'll be here at night."

Outside, they parted company in the driveway. Michelle caught the corner of her mouth between her teeth as she started her car and watched him back his Jaguar out onto the street. "What a mess," she uttered aloud. "What a stupid, stupid mess. Why did you let yourself fall in love with him, you ninny?"

CHAPTER NINE

Tuesday afternoon, as Jon was trying to reach Michelle on the phone, his investigator entered his office. "Hi, Doug. Sit down. I won't be long." He motioned Doug Bennington to a chair and leaned back in his own, waiting for Debbie to answer. She didn't. Instead, Michelle answered the office phone herself.

"Micki, Jon here. This is a surprise. I expected Debbie to answer."

"She had to go out for a few minutes."

"I told you, neither one of you should do anything alone."

"She just went next door" was Michelle's cool answer. "I presume you wanted to speak to me? Or maybe you were going to ask Debbie for a date and chase her for a while?"

"Funny, very funny, Micki," Jon drawled, running his fingers through his sandy hair. "No, I didn't want to talk to Debbie. I want to talk to you."

"About Doris?"

"No, about us."

"There is no us, Jon."

"Says you. I say different, and I think we should

talk some more. So let me take you out to dinner tonight."

"No, thank you. I'm planning to make beef stew at home."

"You can make that tomorrow evening. Tonight let's go to a nice restaurant and—"

"No, Jon. I told you, our relationship's strictly professional now."

He rolled his eyes. "God, Micki, you are the most stubborn—"

"I'm really pretty busy here, Jon. If that's all you wanted—"

"Yeah, that's all for now. But I warn you: You haven't heard the last of this."

"You'll be wasting your time and mine. 'Bye."

"Good-bye," he said disgustedly.

In Chapel Hill, Michelle smiled slightly. Revenge could be sweet, and she certainly seemed to have him going. Maybe now he'd realize he wasn't absolutely irresistible to all women.

In Raleigh, leaning forward in his swivel chair, Jon banged the receiver down in its cradle. When he looked over at Doug Bennington, he found the investigator grinning. He frowned. "Something amuse you?"

"Just glad to know I'm not the only one who has trouble with women," the tall lanky man replied. "I could tell you stories about my wife—but never mind that. I assume Micki is Michelle Vance, the expert on battered women in the Keaton case?"

"That's the one?"

"You're living with her now."

Jon was surprised. "How did you know that?"

Doug shrugged. "I'm a detective. You can't keep many secrets from me."

"I didn't know you were investigating me," Jon said wryly. "Yes, I'm living with her. I'm going to spend every night in her house until the Keaton trial is over."

"Wanting to protect her isn't your only reason for staying, though, is it?"

"There are personal reasons, but I think I'd better keep those to myself. You already know too much about me," Jon said with a smile. "Now tell me, any leads on Vincent Keaton's mistress? Are you any closer to finding out who she is?"

"Not really. I've been watching his hospital room, and he has a steady stream of women visitors—most of them relatively young and comely. I've checked them all out. Some are married, some are single. As of now, I can't say any one of them is more likely than the others to be his mistress. Could be he has more than one."

"Wouldn't surprise me," Jon said, thoughtfully tapping his fingertips against his jaw. "Okay, keep on it. You never know what you might find out. Now, about the harassment of everybody involved in Doris Keaton's defense. Do you have anything we could use to prove that her husband's responsible for it? Any idea who he hired to do his dirty work for him?"

"Not yet. In a not-quite-legal way I managed to get a peek at his bank records," Doug said, with an it's-better-if-you-don't-know-how smile. "He hasn't written any large checks to anyone since he's been hospitalized, but there was a written authorization for a ten-thousand-dollar withdrawal from his savings account. I imagine he paid the thug in cash, or one of his mistresses did."

"If we could only identify her," Jon mused. "Well, keep on it. Maybe we'll get lucky."

"How's it going for you?" Doug asked. "Did you talk to Vincent Keaton's softball teammates?"

"Yeah. Three agreed to testify that he behaves violently at times. The rest didn't want to get involved. The testimony of the three will help me a little in my defense of Doris but not enough, I'm sorry to say. Getting mad at an umpire during the heat of a game doesn't mean you're capable of beating your wife."

"You'll make the case for Mrs. Keaton somehow. You almost always come through for your clients."

"Almost always isn't good enough. I want to get all my clients acquitted."

"Nobody can win every time." Doug rose to his feet somewhat clumsily. He wasn't a perfect physical specimen by any means, but he had an incredibly sharp mind. "Is that all for today, Jon?"

"Yes. Thanks for the briefing."

Doug started out of the office, then stopped to look back. "Good luck with your Micki."

Jon blew out his breath. "I'll need luck. Women! Can't live with them, can't live without them."

"Ain't that the truth?" the lanky investigator said, chuckling as he opened the door and left.

After Doug was gone, Jon thought about the Keaton case for a while before his thoughts returned to Michelle. Such a stubborn woman! Obviously it was difficult for her to trust any man. How could he convince her that he hadn't used her? Flowers! The idea made him smile. If he took her flowers tonight, maybe she would consider them a suitable peace offering.

But the dozen long-stemmed red roses didn't help his cause one bit. Michelle opened the long white box and looked at the flowers. "Pretty. Thanks" was all she said, taking the roses out and placing them in a vase with water. Then she placed the vase in the center of the kitchen table—deliberately, he knew; it would keep them from seeing each other when they had dinner. Muttering a mild curse, he stalked into the living room while she started to prepare the beef stew. He didn't even bother to offer his help. He was tired of her attitude. If she wanted to sulk forever simply because he had been a little inconsiderate, he would damned well let her. Apologizing was getting mighty boring.

The dinner they shared later was hardly relaxing. Michelle played it cool. Jon said very little. She sensed something had changed. Revenge could be sweet, but sometimes it's carried too far. She had a feeling he had had enough of being made to feel guilty. Or maybe he just didn't care about winning her back. She wasn't sure exactly what he felt, but she knew she couldn't back down now. Oh, no—she wanted him to know in no uncertain terms that she had enough respect for herself to expect him to be considerate of her feelings.

Unable to see her face because of the vaseful of roses between them, Jon wearied of their feeble attempts at conversation about impersonal topics. Finally, he thrust the vase to the side of the table and glowered at her. "If we can't find anything better to talk about, why don't we just be quiet?"

"Suits me just fine," she retorted, then took a bite of stew, which tasted like sawdust in her mouth.

The meal was a bust for Jon, too. He merely picked at the stew, and after a while he gave up on eating and excused himself to pour a gin and tonic, which he carried to the living room. He did return to the kitchen to help Michelle with the dishes, but not even sharing this chore alleviated the silence between them.

Winnie seemed to catch their mood. After wandering around the kitchen for a while, getting no response to her fretting meowing, she finally slunk down the basement stairs.

"Guess I'll read my book," Michelle announced when the kitchen was tidied. She glanced at Jon. "What are you going to do?"

"Mind if I watch TV?"

"Be my guest."

Treating each other like strangers, they went into the living room, where he turned the television on to a station showing a documentary about the Vietnam War. With one leg tucked under her, she sat at the opposite end of the sofa from him and picked up her book. She tried to read but couldn't concentrate. She saw the words on the pages but couldn't absorb them. And it was an excellent novel, too. But tonight she just couldn't get into the story. After an hour of trying, she gave up and went to take a bath. "Good night," she said brusquely, heading for her room.

When he heard her door shut, he stared at the uncomfortable sofa, wondering if he would ever get the kinks out of his back after sleeping night after night on such a torturous piece of furniture.

"Dammit to hell, Micki! Why do you have to be so difficult? Women!" he muttered as he switched off the light and made his way in the darkness to his make-shift bed.

Thursday was frantic in Michelle's office. Two battered women sought her help; one brought along three children. With Debbie's help and many phone calls, Michelle managed to get them into safe houses, where they could stay at least a month while trying to find jobs to support themselves. She also set up appointments to counsel them.

By six o'clock in the evening, Debbie was jittery. "I was supposed to meet Bobby an hour ago. He must be having a fit by now," she told Michelle. "Do you think we could finish these files tomorrow?"

"I don't think so. Tomorrow's appointments are back-to-back all day." Michelle smiled understandingly. "But you go on and meet Bobby anyway. I'll finish up here by myself."

Debbie hesitated. "But I thought your Jon said we should stay together. Who'll walk you to your car if I leave now?"

"He's not 'my Jon,' and I think he's being overly cautious. What could possibly happen to me between this office and my car? I park just down the street, which is well-lighted and crowded with students in the evening."

"That's true," Debbie murmured, nodding. "Then you're sure you'll be okay?"

"Of course I will. Go on now and meet Bobby."

"I can't wait to see him tonight. I think he's finally

going to give me an engagement ring," Debbie called out excitedly as she departed.

Unfortunately, when Michelle had finished updating clients' files an hour later, it was raining hard outside. Switching off the lights in the office, she went out and locked the door. She realized that at the university the rain had driven most of the students into their dorms. The sidewalk was practically deserted. Across the street a couple of people braved the inclement weather, but her side of the street seemed empty. Lifting her briefcase over her head to serve as an umbrella, she walked toward her car.

Immediately after she started out, she heard the footsteps behind her. Her heart began to hammer; suddenly, she knew she was in danger. Glancing back over her shoulder, she saw a man gaining rapidly on her. She ran to her car, flung open the door, and got in behind the wheel. She moved swiftly to lock both her door and the one on the passenger side. Half sobbing, she dug her keys out of her purse. In the rearview mirror she saw the man who was after her. He was a huge dark shadow; she couldn't see his face.

"Start! Start!" she begged as she turned the key in the ignition and tapped her foot against the gas pedal. "Oh please, don't stall on me now."

The car cooperated. She put it in gear and sped away from the curb with a squealing of tires.

She was still shaking when she arrived at her house ten minutes later. But when Jon leaped up from the sofa and approached her, concern written on his lean face, she tried to seem perfectly composed. "Where

154

have you been?" he asked anxiously. "I've been waiting for you for over an hour."

"I had some files to catch up on."

That was when he noticed how shaky she was. "You're trembling, Micki. What's happened?"

"N-nothing."

"Don't lie. Tell me the truth."

"Some man followed me when I left my office, that's all. I got to my car before he could catch up with me. And now I'm here, no harm done."

"So I presume Debbie's all right, too?"

"Debbie wasn't with me. She was already late for a date with her fiancé, so I let her go before I left. It was important to her; she was sure he had her engagement ring." Michelle smiled. "I hope he doesn't disappoint her tonight." She took off her suit jacket. "I'm roasting Cornish hens for dinner. Hope you like them."

"To hell with Cornish hens!" he muttered, his hands closing over her shoulders, feeling a great desire to shake her as his eyes hardened and narrowed. "Are you crazy, woman? Didn't I tell you to stay with Debbie from morning till evening? But you let her leave the office before you did, got followed, and could have been—"

"But nothing happened. Maybe it was my imagination. Maybe the man wasn't even following me."

"But you got the impression he was?"

"Yeah, sure, but—"

"Then he probably was," Jon said heatedly, actually shaking her a little. "If you let Debbie leave you alone again, I'll—"

"You'll what?" she asked through clenched teeth.

"Turn me over your knee? You're manhandling me right now, and you know I won't put up with that."

"Do you know how impossible you can be, Micki?"

"No, and I don't care. Just let me go."

"Dammit, woman, I'm just thinking about your safety!" he murmured, hauling her into his arms. "I don't want anything to happen to you."

"I'll be more careful. Now let go."

"I don't think I can do that," he said softly, his breath stirring her hair. "In fact, I don't really think you want me to let you go."

"Jon, I—"

"Stop fighting me." With a fingertip beneath her chin, he tilted her head back so he could see her face. "We both knew this was inevitable when I moved in here. We want each other."

"Oh, no. Don't you dare—"

"Hush," he whispered, then kissed her.

Michelle resisted only a moment. Then the anger she had felt seemed somehow to fuel her passion. It exploded in her as his mouth took arousing possession of hers. Winding her arms upward around his neck, she kissed him back, delighting in being close to him once again. When he slipped his hands beneath her suit jacket and cupped her breasts, she strained against him. Heat flowed through her body.

"See what we've been missing since I came back from New York?" he said softly. "Why don't we continue this in the bedroom?"

"I may be crazy," she murmured against his smooth, tanned neck. "And I may hate myself later for letting this happen."

"You won't." Releasing her, he took her by the hand and led her down the short hall.

When he sat down on the edge of the bed and looked up at her, she was puzzled. "What are you doing?"

He moved her back a short distance. "I want to sit here and watch you undress."

She smiled. "I'm not a stripper."

"I want you to for me. Would a little music help you along?"

"I'm not that much of a ham," she retorted, then laughed at a memory of their other night together. "At least this beats your gorilla suit idea."

He grinned. "Then start taking it off. Take it all off."

"Will you stop? You're going to make me self-conscious!"

"You never have to be shy with me."

Yet she was, a little, as she removed her jacket and skirt. He was watching her so intently, with such a sensuous expression, that her fingers shook a bit as she undid the buttons of her pearl-gray blouse. After taking it off, she let it slip through her fingers to drift to the floor with a silken whisper. She stepped out of her shoes, then removed her half slip, lowering it down over hips and stepping out of it, aware every second of Jon's eyes on her.

"Now comes the hard part," she murmured, bending forward slightly, her hair falling forward to conceal the pink color rising in her cheeks. "It's impossible to get out of pantyhose gracefully."

"You'll do fine. The show's getting better and better."

After she hobbled first on one foot, then the other, the pantyhose were off. Now she was clad only in her pink bra and matching panties. She hesitated.

"Come on now, take it all off," he coached. "I want to get what I paid for."

"You didn't pay me anything."

"Want me to give you a dollar?"

"Is that all you think this is worth?" she asked, pretending to be highly insulted. "One lousy dollar?"

"I only offered a dollar as a token payment because no amount of money could pay for this incredible show."

"Sweet talker."

"Yes. And right now I'm trying to talk you out of all your clothes, so keep going."

Their light banter eased her shyness, and she smiled faintly at him as she unhooked her bra and slowly peeled the lace cups away from her breasts. Her pulse raced when she saw hot desire glint in his eyes.

When she dropped the bra and her hands started downward, he reached out to put his own around her trim waist. "Let me do this part," he said, his voice gruff as he slipped his fingertips beneath the waistband of her panties.

He took them off very, very slowly. She finally said, "You're taking a very long time doing that."

"Just enjoying the scenery along the way. You have fantastic legs. In fact, all of you is fantastic."

"I'm glad you think so," she said, smoothing his thick hair with one hand as he bent down in front of her. At last she was naked. He raised back up and leaned forward to press his lips against her belly button.

"Hold on—not so fast, mister. Before we start the serious stuff, you have to undress for me."

"No problem." He rose to his feet and sat her down on the edge of the bed. He started unbuttoning his shirt; his jacket and tie were already off. "One of my fantasies is to become a male stripper."

"It is not."

"No, it isn't. I was just hoping the thought would excite you."

"I'm already excited. And if you don't get undressed soon, I'm going to get the idea you're stalling."

Quickly he finished unbuttoning his shirt and took it off. He kicked off his shoes, then removed his trousers. After pulling off his socks, his shorts joined the growing pile of clothes on the floor. Without an iota of bashfulness, he straightened up and stretched his arms out. "Ta-da. How did I do?"

"Well, you were certainly fast after you finally got started," she told him, almost laughing. "I think the best strippers work at a slower tempo to heighten the anticipation."

"So I'll never strip for a living. Another fantasy shot to hell," he murmured, moving closer, his eyes wandering lazily over her. With one hand, he gently parted her legs. He moved between them and lowered her back onto the bed. He leaned over her, cupping her face in his hands and grazing his thumbs over her lusciously soft lips. "Now, Micki, it's time to start the 'serious stuff,' as you put it."

"Yes, it's time now," she whispered, more madly in love with him than she had ever been. Her lips sought his as she lightly stepped her fingertips over his broad muscular chest. When the weight of his upper body pushed her down into the softness of the mattress, she clasped her arms around his waist.

To Jon, it seemed like years since they had touched each other this way. He needed to kiss and caress every inch of her, to inhale the sweet fresh fragrance of her creamy skin. When she had come into the house tonight and told him about the man who had followed her, he had been overwhelmed with fear for her. She had become tremendously important to him. If something were to happen to her because he had involved her in the Keaton case, he wouldn't ever be able to forgive himself. But now she was safely in his arms, and he held her as if he'd never let her go. He buried his face in her scented hair.

Turning her head toward him, Michelle initiated more long passionate kisses, then ardently whispered, "Jon," again and again as his stroking fingers left her throbbing breasts to wander downward and explore her most feminine warmth. His lips followed the trail his hand had blazed, and she thought she might faint in the throes of the pleasure he bestowed. With her own hands and lips she thoroughly explored his virile body too as their passion grew. Then her physical need, enhanced by her love for him, became too intense.

"Take me, Jon!" she breathed. "Love me now."

160

"Soon, baby."

"Now, now! I can't wait. I want you."

"Ah, I want you, too, so much," he groaned. "I can't wait, either." Parting her long legs wider, he moved with a tender thrust inside her, deeper and deeper.

They made love once with wild abandon, then again more slowly, whispering sweet nothings to each other. It was wonderful for them both, both ways. Hot quick passion had its advantages, but so did slow burning desire.

Afterward, they lay in each other's arms, content in the magical warmth they had created together. Michelle snuggled close to him and kissed his chest.

He lightly rubbed his chin against her head. "Well, do you?"

"Do I what?"

"Hate yourself for letting this happen?"

"No," she answered, smiling. "No, I'm glad, in fact."

"Then you forgive me?"

"Yes, I do, but I still think it was inconsiderate of you not to call me when you were in New York."

"I've admitted that's true, and I've just done my best to show you how considerate I can be."

"Um, that's true. I guess we've made up."

They snuggled closer and continued to make up for some time, until finally their passion was sated.

Awhile later, while he was still holding Michelle in his arms, Jon told her, "Doris Keaton's trial starts next week. Wednesday we start selecting the jury."

"Is she ready to face trial yet?"

"Dr. Evans, her psychiatrist, seems to think so."

"When will I have to testify?"

"Probably the first day of the actual trial. I plan to put you on the stand third, after Doris's sister Anna and Dr. Evans. The prosecutor makes his case first, of course, but he's told us he only plans to call Vincent Keaton. His testimony shouldn't take long, so we should get to yours that same day. Just remember to try to look a little older so the jury will take you seriously."

"Okay," she murmured. She smiled when Winnie pushed the door open and scooted across the floor to jump up onto the bed. When Jon put his hand out to pet Winnie, Michelle quickly caught it and pulled it back. "Don't touch her until she's been fed. Remember? She gets nasty and spits when she's hungry."

Winnie meowed loudly, jumped back down off the bed, and trotted out into the hall as if trying to lead them to the kitchen where her food was kept.

"She's obviously starved," Michelle said with a grin. "How about you?"

"I'm famished, too."

"It's going to take too long to bake the Cornish hens. Maybe we should have something else."

"Let's order pizza."

"Great. I want lots of pepperoni."

"And extra cheese," he said, hugging her close and kissing her forehead. "I'm glad you provoked me into grabbing you tonight. Now I can sleep in this bed with you from now on and save my poor back from that awful couch."

The joke disappointed her, and she bit her lower lip.

162

"Always with the wisecracks, aren't you? Can't you ever be truly romantic?"

Sensing her change of mood, he got serious. "Did you ever consider the possibility that I make wisecracks to mask insecurity?"

She looked up at him. "What in the world could make you insecure?"

"Maybe I'm as afraid of getting seriously involved with someone as you are," he said somberly, playing with her hair. "Maybe I just hide that fear better than you do."

She didn't answer. He had it all wrong. True, she had been afraid of serious involvement before she met him, but now things were different. Now she yearned for a permanent relationship with him. But if he was as wary of making a commitment as she had once been, could their relationship ever lead to something lasting? Much as she hated to admit it to herself, it didn't look promising, considering his current feelings.

CHAPTER TEN

Wednesday's jury selection went smoothly, and the actual trial was slated to begin on Thursday. That morning Jon insisted Michelle ride to the courthouse with him.

"But you don't think anything's going to happen between here and there," she asked while brushing her hair, "do you?"

"I just don't know. If someone is really determined to stop you from testifying in Doris's behalf, anything might happen."

"Well, I think it's all been a big bluff from the beginning. Somebody's been trying to scare us into dropping the case. I doubt they ever planned to actually harm us."

"Maybe. But it's better to be safe than sorry, so ride to court with me. Humor me."

"Oh, okay. But what if I finish my testimony early and want to go to my office?"

"You can call Debbie and have her come pick you up." Jon glanced at his wristwatch. "You about ready to leave? I don't want to be late. Judges don't care for tardy attorneys."

"I just have to do my hair," she said, pulling her auburn tresses tight back from her face and winding them into a chignon, which she secured with pins on the nape of her neck. Then she put on her driving glasses and turned away from the vanity mirror to face Jon. "Well, do I look older?"

His appraising gaze swept over her, then he shook his head and smiled. "Not very much older."

She grimaced. "I hope I'll be able to convince the jury I know what I'm talking about." She smoothed her skirt with her hands. "And what about this suit? Is it okay?"

"It's fine. Professional without being too severe. Now try to relax, get your purse, and let's get out of here." After they were in his Jaguar and on the way, he abruptly said, "You're nervous, aren't you?"

"I guess I am a little. No, that's a lie," she admitted, clutching her hands tightly together on her lap. "I'm very nervous. I've never testified in court before, and I keep thinking that if I mess up somehow or don't seem convincing, Doris is going to be in a lot of trouble."

Jon reached over to pat her left arm reassuringly. "You're not going to mess up, and you'll be convincing. Just answer the questions with the facts."

"I'm not worried about your questions. It's the prosecutor's that concern me."

"He'll be tough on you, that's true. Just remember you're an expert on battered women. He isn't."

"I'll try to. If I'm nervous this morning, I wonder how poor Doris must be feeling?"

"I called her sister while you were getting dressed,"

Jon told her. "Anna said Doris is holding up pretty well. Dr. Evans gave her a mild tranquilizer."

"Wish I'd thought of having my doctor do the same for me."

"It's the thinking about it that's bothering you." Jon squeezed her arm and smiled again. "Once you're on the stand, you'll be cool as a cucumber, I'm sure. I have confidence in you."

"That makes me feel better," she said, smiling back. "Thanks, Jon."

"Don't mention it."

When they reached the courthouse several minutes later and found a parking space, Michelle was amazed at the crowd that had gathered outside the doors. Jon came around to open her door and she got out of the car, and she shook her head disbelievingly. "I knew people were interested in this case, but I didn't think so many of them would come to the trial."

"Probably most of them are press. Vincent Keaton is a best-selling author, and his wife is accused of trying to kill him. I'm afraid the trial's going to get a lot of publicity."

"Just what Doris needs," Michelle murmured sympathetically as she and Jon went up the courthouse steps and pushed through the crowd.

The trial started promptly with opening statements from Jon and the prosecution. Jon was very eloquent. Then the assistant DA, Arthur Clinton, called Vincent Keaton to the stand. He was still wearing a sling on his left arm from the shoulder wound he'd suffered.

Michelle, sitting just behind the defense table, had seen Keaton once before, when he'd done an

166

autographing at the bookstore next door to her office. She had forgotten what he'd looked like, however, and now she knew why. He was ordinary looking, nondescript. He looked like just what he was—a professor-turned-author. He even acted a trifle absent-minded as he took the oath and swore to tell the whole truth. There was no sign that that bland face masked a sadist inside. But from Doris, Michelle had learned what he was capable of doing. For her, he was slime.

And his testimony was one long, atrocious lie. He said that several weeks before the shooting, he'd become aware of the fact that his wife was seeing another man. Jon immediately objected, noting that the prosecution had absolutely no evidence that would prove Doris was having an affair. The judge ruled in favor of his objection, so the prosecutor went directly to the night of the shooting. When Vincent Keaton swore Doris had been waiting in the house to shoot him, that he'd never even touched his softball bat that evening, Michelle turned up her nose with disgust. But Jon couldn't shake the man's story on cross-examination. He was an excellent liar, and not a bad actor, either. When he finally left the stand, he looked over at Doris and shook his head as if he couldn't understand her behavior. Michelle felt like smacking him. Doris trembled and looked away, that awful haunted look briefly returning to her eyes. The prosecution rested.

Michelle was called to the stand after the noon recess, following Anna and Dr. Evans. Jon had been right. The moment she laid her hand on the Bible and took the oath, she felt calm and confident in her expertise. Answering Jon's questions, she tried to establish

167

in the minds of the jury that battered women share the same experiences, even strikingly similar upbringings. She felt her testimony was quite effective. But then it was assistant DA Arthur Clinton's turn at bat. He was a pain from start to finish. "I believe you're telling the court that, in your opinion, Doris Keaton fits the pattern of the typical abused woman" were his first words. "Is that right, Ms. Vance?"

"Yes, it is. Her sheltered childhood, her deference to authority figures—especially men; her failed first mar—"

"That's fine; we've already heard all that," he interrupted caustically. "You seem to have a great many facts at your disposal. I assume there have been studies done on abused women?"

"Of course, several."

"Published studies?"

"Yes."

"Even books on the subject?"

"Yes, a few."

"Did you ever actually see Vincent Keaton abuse Doris Keaton, the defendant?"

"Well, of course not," Michelle answered honestly. "I never met Mrs. Keaton until after the shooting."

"Then you don't really know that he abused her, do you? You're only going on what she told you he did. Is that right?"

"She does fit the—"

"Couldn't the defendant have read some of those books and simply made up a story she knew you'd believe?"

Jon jumped up. "Objection, Your Honor. Mr. Clinton's badgering the witness, not allowing her to answer his questions."

Once again the judge ruled in his favor.

The prosecutor apologized profusely and quite insincerely, in Michelle's opinion. She was beginning to feel a distinct dislike for the man.

"Let me ask you again: After reading a book or books about the typical battered woman, couldn't the defendant have fabricated a story you'd believe?"

"I don't think she did that."

"Just answer yes or no, please. Isn't it possible she might have done that?"

"Well, yes, but what you don't understand is that the first time I met Mrs. Keaton after the shooting, she was afraid to leave her bedroom at her sister's house. And she was so afraid of all men, she couldn't even bear to be alone with her attorney, Mr. Wyatt. Her husband had terrorized her that much."

Arthur Clinton was livid. "I move to strike the witness's last statement from the record and the jury be advised to ignore it."

The judge concurred.

Clinton renewed his attack. "Now I ask you, Ms. Vance, isn't it possible that the defendant, Mrs. Keaton, was putting on a brilliant act for your benefit when you first met her?"

"If she was acting, then she deserves an Academy Award for her performance," Michelle answered brusquely, getting a pleased smile from Jon because of her response.

"Just answer yes or no. Is it possible she was putting on an act?"

Michelle glanced up at the judge. "Your Honor—"

"Answer the question, Ms. Vance," he admonished.

"Well then, yes, anything's possible, I guess. She might have been acting, but I—"

"No more questions." The assistant DA cut her off, gave her a smarmy smile, then strolled back to his table.

As Michelle left the stand, feeling her testimony had been picked to pieces, the judge adjourned court for the day. She waited for Jon as he spoke briefly to Doris, who was then quickly whisked out a side door by her sister and brother-in-law. Together, Jon and Michelle ran the gauntlet of reporters waiting outside. Jon refused to answer any questions as they made their way to his car. Once they were safely inside, he quickly drove away from the courthouse.

"Oh God, I blew it," she groaned, closing her eyes and resting her head against the back of the seat. "Didn't I?"

"No, you didn't. I think you did very well."

Her eyes flew open, darted over to him. "You mean you think the jury believes Doris was abused by Vincent?"

"Not exactly. Not yet. But the jury believes that you believe she was, and that counts for something. You were very convincing, Micki."

"I don't know how. That Clinton's a bastard."

"Oh, Art's not a bad fellow. We play racquetball once in a while."

"You're kidding!"

"No, I'm not. Art and I are friends outside the courtroom. In it we're opponents—both of us just do-

170

ing our jobs." Jon smiled at her. "Besides, he could've been a lot harder on you. This is one time old Art dropped the ball."

She frowned, confused. "What do you mean?"

"I mean, he should have known I moved in with you. He could've asked you if our personal relationship hadn't influenced your testimony, insinuating to the jury that you might be lying for my client."

Michelle gasped; her face went deathly pale. "Oh, my God. I never thought of that."

"I did."

"Then why didn't you warn me he might know we're living together and ask me about it?"

"Because I knew you'd be too tense on the stand if you were wondering if he was going to bring up our relationship. By the way, if he had, how would you have answered?"

She thought for several seconds as her shock began to abate. "I think I would have said you moved in with me because Vincent Keaton had hired someone to try to scare me into deciding not to testify for Doris. That you moved in to protect me. That's the truth, too."

"Perfect answer. You're one hell of a woman, Micki," he said sincerely, reaching over to cup the nape of her neck with his hand. "I knew I was right to have confidence in you. Now, take your hair down, will you please? With it up like that in that tight bun, you look like a schoolmarm from the Old West."

Smiling lovingly at him, she removed the pins from her confined hair. It cascaded in soft waves down around her shoulders.

"Better," he murmured approvingly. "Much better."

She leaned across the gear console between their seats and brushed a kiss across his right cheek.

Michelle had thought that testifying at the trial would end the threatening phone calls. It didn't. She received another one Saturday morning while Jon was at his Raleigh office, picking up important papers he needed over the weekend.

"You wouldn't listen, would you?" the raspy voice said this time. "Now you're going to have to pay for testifying for Doris Keaton. You're going to be very sorry, bitch."

"Buzz off, pervert," she replied coolly, although she was trembling. She slammed the receiver down. She wearily massaged the back of her neck. "Damn, damn, damn."

A second later the front bell rang. She nearly jumped out of her skin. "Who's there?" she called out, approaching the door slowly. "Who is it?"

"It's me, Debbie."

"Oh, thank goodness," murmured Michelle, fumbling with the locks, then opening the door fast. "Come on in."

Debbie stared at her. "When you asked who I was, you sounded as if you were expecting Dracula or Frankenstein to answer. What's the matter?"

"I just had another one of those damned threatening phone calls."

"That doesn't make sense. Why warn you not to testify when you've already done it?"

"The man's changed the threat. Now he tells me he's going to get me because of what I did."

"He's stopped calling me. I wish he'd leave you alone, too." Debbie looked around the living room. "Where's Jon? Don't be surprised I asked that. I know he's staying here with you."

"Not much gets past you, Deb," Michelle said wryly, motioning toward the sofa. "Let's sit down. Can I offer you some coffee?"

"No thanks."

"Jon had to go to his office to pick something up," Michelle said, joining Debbie on the sofa and smoothing her gray slacks. "He should be back soon. So what brings you to this neck of the woods? I thought you always did your shopping on Saturday mornings."

"I'm on my way now, but I had to stop and show you this." Debbie proudly held out her left hand and smiled, beaming. "Bobby finally came through. I knew he would if I prodded him long enough. He gave it to me last night. I was about to call and tell you, but it was getting late. Well, what do you think of it?"

"It's beautiful, Deb," Michelle said sincerely, admiring the diamond solitaire on her finger. "Really beautiful. And you look so excited and happy. I'm glad. Have you and Bobby set the date yet?"

"What do you want, miracles? I had a hard enough time persuading him to make the engagement official." Debbie regarded Michelle thoughtfully. "Think you'll be getting one of these soon?"

"From Jon, you mean?"

"Of course Jon. Who else would I mean, Attila the Hun? Is he going to ask you to marry him soon?"

"I very seriously doubt it."

"But you're in love with him."

"How can you be sure?" Michelle asked. "I've never told you that."

"Didn't have to. Like you said, nothing much gets by me. Is he in love with you, too?"

"You should know the answer to that. You know everything."

"But I hardly ever get to see Jon. You I see at least five days a week. So what do you think?" Debbie persisted. "Does he love you?"

"I don't know, either."

"Why don't you ask him?"

"Because I'm not as direct as you are," Michelle said with a rueful smile. "I don't think I could ever be."

"Want me to ask him for you?"

"Don't you dare, Deb!"

"Kidding, just kidding," Debbie said impishly, then rose to her feet to leave. "Better hit the road now."

As Michelle was walking her to the door, Jon returned, sweeping into the house with a quick hello to the receptionist. He headed straight for Michelle, lifted her up, and swung her around the living room three times before putting her back down. "Something great happened while I was at my office," he said. "I got a phone call from New York."

"Oh, who called?"

"A woman."

"What are you talking about?" Michelle asked, thoroughly confused. "What woman?"

174

He smiled at both her and Debbie. "Vincent Keaton's first wife."

"What?" they cried simultaneously.

"What do you mean, first wife?" Michelle added. "Doris never told me he had been married before."

"She didn't know," Jon explained. "I stopped by Anna's house on my way home, and when I told Doris about the woman's call, she was flabbergasted. Vincent had never even mentioned being married before. Doris thought she was his first wife."

"Incredible," Debbie murmured. "What a weird man."

"His ex-wife," Michelle said. "Why did she call you?"

"Her name is Jess Masters. She remarried, too. Seems she's been touring Europe for the past couple months and didn't know Vincent had been shot until she came back to the States. When she learned that Doris was going to be tried for attempted murder, she had a talk with her present husband, and they agreed that she should come forward with the truth. She's willing to come down here and testify that Vincent abused her, too. She only took his abuse for a month before she left him, but he did treat her the same way he treated Doris."

"Hooray!" Debbie cheered. "Now Doris will be acquitted for sure."

"Not so fast," Michelle cautioned, looking up at Jon. "After Jess Masters testifies and the jury hears that she left Vincent after only one month, won't they wonder why Doris didn't just leave him, too?"

"I considered that possibility. But we have an ace in

the hole. When I asked Mrs. Masters a few questions, she told me that she was raised by her parents to be very independent, not docile and helpless, as Doris was conditioned from birth to be. I think I can convince the jury that Jess Masters had to leave Vincent because he abused her and that Doris was too afraid to leave for the very same reason. Acquittal's not a sure thing, of course; it never is, but we do have a stronger case now."

Once again Jon picked Michelle up and spun her around. "We should celebrate. What would you like to do?"

Debbie coughed lightly to gain their attention, then gave them a little wave. "Three's a crowd, and I know when to make an exit, so I'll be off now."

Michelle walked her out onto the porch. "Thanks for coming by to show me your ring. I hope you and Bobby will be very happy together."

"Yeah, me too. I think he is."

Michelle frowned. "Run that past me again, please."

"I think Jon's in love with you, too."

"Probably wishful thinking on your part."

"But—"

"Just go shopping," Michelle said with a smile. "Like you said, three's a crowd."

After Debbie walked down the porch steps and across the lawn to her car, Michelle went back into the house and was immediately embraced by Jon again. His excitement was contagious; she was quickly caught up in it and smiled happily up at him. "Okay, so you want to celebrate. But what can we do? It's too cool today for another picnic. Let's see now. I guess we could go somewhere really nice for lunch. Order champagne."

"We could do that, too. Right now, I'd hoped you had something else in mind," he whispered in her left ear as his hands wandered up under her white sweater, warming her breasts. "I have something else in mind, Micki."

"Um, I can tell," she whispered back, withdrawing from his arms to lead him to the bedroom. The phone call she had received completely skipped her mind; much later, when she did remember and told him about it, she was glad she had forgotten for a while. The wondrous hours they shared in bed were so romantic. She wouldn't have wanted anything unpleasant to lessen their delight in each other.

CHAPTER ELEVEN

Michelle didn't attend the trial on Friday because she had her own work to do. On Monday, however, she went into the courtroom. After Jon called several character witnesses to testify on Doris's behalf, he planned to put Doris herself on the stand. Michelle wanted to be there to provide any moral support she could.

Answering Jon's questions, Doris told what a nightmare her marriage to Vincent had been. Michelle kept one eye on the jury box. About half the jurors seemed sympathetic to her story; the other half looked skeptical. But Michelle knew something they didn't: Jon had a surprise witness to spring on the prosecution. Surely Vincent's ex-wife's sworn testimony that he had abused her would sway every jury member into voting for acquittal.

On cross-examination, assistant DA Arthur Clinton questioned Doris ruthlessly. Yet she held up and answered his questions quietly and truthfully. Michelle was proud of her. Although she was obviously still somewhat intimidated by Vincent and wouldn't look directly at him as he sat in the gallery, she was a stronger, more self-confident woman than the one Michelle had first met.

After the lunch recess, when Arthur Clinton finally finished grilling Doris, Jon sent the prosecution reeling by calling Jess Masters to the stand. Glancing back over her shoulder to the third row across the aisle, where Vincent Keaton sat, Michelle saw him stiffen and go slightly pale when he heard the name and saw the woman. Obviously he sensed her gaze and glanced over at her. For an instant she could see intense hatred and cruelty flash in his eyes. She shuddered inwardly, knowing now why Doris was so afraid of him.

After Jon questioned Jess Master extensively, the prosecution cross-examined her, but her answers remained rock solid and unshakable. Michelle thought she was an extremely effective witness. After she was allowed to leave the stand, Jon told the judge, "Defense rests, Your Honor."

His closing arguments and those of Arthur Clinton followed. Michelle thought the assistant district attorney's arguments were outrageously lame. Surely it was now obvious to the jury that Doris hadn't been planning to murder Vincent when he came home that night. Surely they knew now that she had only shot him because he had come after her with a baseball bat.

After instructing the jurors on the various verdicts they might make, the judge had them sequestered for their deliberations. Then everyone in the courtroom rose when he got up to retire to his chambers. A babble of voices broke out, and Michelle leaned across the railing in front of her to hug Doris. "Oh, you were

179

great on the stand, Doris," she said. "And with Jess Masters's testimony, you've got it made."

"Let's just say our chances for acquittal are very good," Jon modified Michelle's enthusiastic assurances. "But you have to remember, Doris. There are twelve individuals on that jury, and it's hard to predict what even one person might think or do. In other words, it's not over until it's over."

"Then I still might have to go to prison?"

"I don't think so, but it's a possibility."

"Oh God, hasn't Vincent done enough to me already?" she muttered, fighting tears and winning. Stiffening her back, she remained dry-eyed.

Michelle had thought the jury would return with an innocent verdict within minutes, but she thought wrong. The jury was out for nearly four hours. The judge returned from his chambers to the bench and was apparently about to adjourn for the day when the bailiff approached and spoke quietly to him.

"The jury has reached a verdict," the judge announced to the still-packed courtroom. "Are counsels for the prosecution and defense present at this time?"

"Yes, Your Honor," Jon and Arthur Clinton said at the same time.

A few minutes later the jury filed back in and took their seats in the box. Only the foreman remained standing. He handed the written verdict to the bailiff, who in turn gave it to the judge, who glanced at it and handed it back.

"Will the defendant please rise?" the judge said.

As Jon stood up with Doris, Michelle clasped her hands tightly together. The suspense was unbearable.

If the bailiff didn't read the verdict aloud soon, she thought she would scream.

At last the bailiff cleared his throat and began. "In the case of the State of North Carolina against Doris Porter Keaton, we the jury find the defendant not guilty."

Michelle dropped back into her seat as all hell broke loose in the courtroom. Anna shouted happily and ran toward Doris as reporters pushed forward, trying to get statements. Michelle saw Doris sag beside Jon; he had to put his arm around her waist to keep her on her feet. Then Anna was there to grab her and hug her. Both women began to cry for joy. Michelle was teary, too, and she noticed that when Jon turned to smile at her, he wasn't totally dry-eyed, either.

"Mrs. Keaton will answer your questions outside on the courthouse steps," he told the horde of reporters trying to get to her. "Please give her a little time to catch her breath."

Most of them ignored him, and a battery of questions were aimed at Doris all at once, creating such a babble that no one's words were understandable.

"I repeat, Mrs. Keaton will answer your questions outside," Jon reiterated firmly, his jaw hardening. "It's either out there in a few minutes, ladies and gentlemen, or not at all."

The members of the press got the message. Grumbling, they started to walk away. Several of the jurors came over to say a few words to Doris, who thanked them profusely for believing her and the witnesses who had testified in her behalf. Assistant DA Arthur Clinton moved from his table over to Jon's, smiled, and shook his hand.

"Did you ever get lucky on this one, Wyatt!" Clinton said with a smile. "If you hadn't put the ex-wife on the stand, it would have been a different story."

"Why don't you just admit it, old pal?" Jon retorted, smiling too. "You simply blew it, Art."

Shrugging, Clinton looked at Michelle, who was now standing. "Sorry I had to be so rough on you on cross-examination, Ms. Vance."

She made a small gesture with one hand. "Jon told me you were just doing your job, Mr. Clinton."

" 'Jon,' is it?" His gaze went back and forth between them a couple of times then became comprehending. "I have a feeling I've missed something here. Is there something going on between you two?"

"Too late to wonder about that now," Jon told him with a grin. "Verdict's in, trial's over."

"I'll be damned," Art Clinton muttered to himself as he slowly walked away.

Michelle and Jon exchanged sneaky smiles; then he gathered his papers off the table to put them in his briefcase. Doris and her sister had begun to compose themselves, and Doris hugged her brother-in-law when he joined them, smiling broadly.

"I knew they'd find you innocent," he said. "You just don't look like a Ma Barker."

Laughing shakily, Doris noticed Michelle and came around the railing that divided the courtroom to hug her, too. "Thank you for helping keep me out of prison. Thank you for everything. My talks with you have made me feel much stronger."

"I'm glad," Michelle murmured, tears filling her eyes again.

"We have to celebrate," Anna said as they walked in a group out of the courtroom. "Mr. Wyatt, I hope you and Michelle will let Doris, Bill, and me take you out to dinner tonight."

Jon stopped in the doorway. "I think we'd better postpone the celebration. We should all leave town for a short while to give Vincent's hot temper a chance to cool down. Doris, your acquittal means people are going to believe he abused you. That's not going to be good for his reputation. It might even damage his relationship with his publisher. I doubt any publisher appreciates an author gaining such notoriety."

All the smiles disappeared; everyone was solemn now. That old look of terror came back into Doris's eyes.

"You're right, Mr. Wyatt," she muttered bleakly. "I know better than anybody how vindictive Vincent can be."

"Yeah, and I saw him stalk out of here after the verdict was read," her brother-in-law said. "His face was red as a beet, and he looked fit to be tied."

"Because now he knows he's going to have to give me a divorce settlement. Mr. Wyatt, will you file for divorce for me, too?"

"I don't handle divorce cases, Doris, but I have a partner who does only that. Her name's Sarah Elderman. Give her a call."

"I will. Thank you," Doris said.

"Tell you what, ladies," her brother-in-law said to both his wife and her sister as they walked down the wide hall. "We'll fly out and spend a few days with my brother Fred in Wyoming. I know he's been awful lonesome since Hilda died. He'll be glad to have our company."

On the courthouse steps the reporters mobbed Doris again. Jon stuck by her side while Michelle waited at the bottom of the stairs. When the members of the press started repeating their questions and Jon could tell that Doris had had as much as she could take, he helped her thread her way down through the pushing and shoving crowd and got her into the car, where her sister and brother-in-law waited. They quickly drove away, and the avid reporters quickly surrounded Jon and Michelle.

"Answer this, counselor," one of them shouted, louder than the others. "Was Doris Keaton's acquittal really a conviction of Vincent for abusing her?"

"I think you could safely say that," he replied, pushing through the circle. "Your viewers and readers are probably going to assume that he batters women. After all, women testified to that. And that's the last question I'm going to answer. Excuse me, ladies and gentlemen."

Cupping Michelle's elbow in his hand, he hurried her to the car. When they were inside, the reporters gave up and scattered. Michelle breathed a sigh of relief then smiled at Jon. She leaned across to lightly kiss his lips.

"Congratulations, counselor," she said softly. "You won a big one."

"But Art was right. I did get lucky. If Vincent's ex-wife hadn't called me, I would never have known she

184

existed. My investigator, Doug Bennington, should have turned up the fact that he'd been married before, but somehow he missed it."

"But all's well that ends well. All that really matters is that Doris is a free woman again. I guess," Michelle qualified her words. She frowned worriedly. "Or do you think she might always be in danger of Vincent's desire for revenge?"

"After he cools down, I think he'll realize he can't harm her without getting into big trouble."

"I hope you're right," Michelle said as he started the car and they drove away from the courthouse. "Do you really think we need to get out of town for a while?"

"I really do. We're leaving tonight. You can get away from work on short notice, can't you?"

"Well, sure. I'll have Debbie put me in for an emergency leave, and she can postpone my appointments. But for how long?"

"A week."

"Where are we going?"

"The Virgin Islands. St. Croix, to be specific. Sound okay to you?"

"It would sound terrific if I could afford it," she said regretfully, thinking of her meager savings account. "But I can't. Maybe we'd better go someplace closer to home and less exotic."

"My treat."

"No, I couldn't let you pay my way."

"Stubborn woman, you're forgetting something. I can put the whole trip for both of us on my expense account since we're being forced to leave town because of a case I handled."

She gave him another smile. "Well, when you put it that way, St. Croix sounds great. I've never been there. Have you?"

"Once. It's a beautiful island."

Excitement surged through her as she anticipated a whole week alone on an island paradise with Jon.

St. Croix was beautiful. Michelle loved it there. The spate of rain every afternoon lessened the humidity in the air, and except for those brief showers the sky remained blue and sun-filled. The meals they were served were all delectable; they danced at night in the moonlight on a tiled terrace and spent their days romping and playing in the sapphire waters of the Caribbean. They made love constantly.

On their last afternoon on the island Jon turned toward Michelle, propping himself up on one elbow on the wide beach towel they shared. She was asleep, her sun-washed auburn hair ablaze with vibrant color in the natural light. Her lips were slightly parted. Her dark brown eyelashes feathered against her cheekbones. A wealth of emotions stole over him as he reached over to trace a gentle fingertip down the bridge of her nose and across her lips.

Disturbed by his arousing touch, she slowly awakened, blinked her eyes, and murmured sleepily, "Hi."

"Hi, yourself, sleepyhead," he murmured back, smiling lazily. "Now get the lead out, woman. This is our last afternoon here. We should be swimming. Instead, you're taking a nap."